The Story of the Stars

HIMANI DESAI

notionpress.com

INDIA · SINGAPORE · MALAYSIA

Hiya

I was walking on a barren street covered with enormous trees at night. Half of the streetlights weren't working. I had no idea where I was and how I ended up there. The scary howling of the wolves shook the core of my heart. A tiny raindrop settled on my hand. When I peered up towards the sky, a long bolt of lightning formed over my head. In a minute, I was completely drenched. I saw an abandoned big house that was in poor shape. The rain was getting worse, and it left me no choice but to go inside. The large wooden door, three times my height, opened magically.

With my first step inside, the fire lamps ignited all at once. I saw a chandelier about the size of my bed was dangling in the middle of the hall. I followed the path of the fire lamps to explore the place more. All of a sudden, the place began to tremble. It widened my eyes after noticing that the marble flooring beneath me was splitting. I ran back to the main door to save myself. On the way, I watched that the crack was racing with me. In a second, it surpassed me, and I fell into it. The next moment, I woke up on my bed with a thrust.

It was just a dream! I consoled myself. I pulled off my comforter and drank water. *I have to stop watching fantasy movies until late at night.* I thought. I stretched my arms and looked around my room. The empty pizza box and coke can were on the floor, next to the laptop. A loud knock on the door scared me. I heard my name, and that was my mother shouting. I hastily put everything in its place and hurried to open the door.

'How many times have I told you not to lock the door if you want to sleep till late?' She threw the complaint before I opened the door fully. 'Weren't you supposed to bring breakfast today?' Before I could express my apology, she complained again.

When I decided to bring the breakfast, she stopped me saying my father had already brought it. I ran down the stairs quickly and saw a plate of *fafda-jalebi*. My father, reading the newspaper, cleared his throat dramatically. I focused on eating, ignoring him.

'Wait, where is Doodle?' I asked, looking around.

'Out for a walk, not like you,' my father taunted.

'Good boy!' I exclaimed, chewing the last bite.

I went in search of Doodle, my two-year-old, cream-white male retriever, a handsome, intelligent, adorable, and highly energetic guy. When I got Doodle as a gift from my parents, he was just two months old. But now the big boy can go for a walk on his own as he is familiar with society's roads.

I knew where to find him. I walked to the society garden and found my furry friend playing with kids. I blew a whistle and sat down on my knees. Doodle looked at me and barked loudly. I threw my hands in the air looking at him running towards me. I clutched his face and poured dozens of kisses. Together we played his favourite game of fetch the ball for half an hour. I never get bored playing with Doodle. The bond with an animal is the purest relationship in the world. There are no complaints or expectations, just a bunch of pure love and happiness. I would say, *love them, don't despise them. Feed them, don't eat them.* That's what they deserve.

At noon, I received a text from Kavya. *School friends are planning to have dinner tonight. You're coming with me, no excuses.* A sudden train of thoughts crossed my mind. *Who is coming? Where are they going to meet? Will I get to see Arnav?* The last time I spotted him on the road was when I was going for shopping with my mother, on scooter. I've just attended one reunion in last two years.

I don't have a long list of friends but I've maintained my true friendship with Kavya. She has been my good friend since the first standard. After my parents, only Kavya is the one who is aware of my introverted nature and never complained. Speaking less and observing more is my top notch quality. My nature has caused me trouble at some points but has saved me too. After completing school, I and Kavya both got admission to the same college but in different fields of engineering. She opted for electrical and I chose civil engineering.

On the list of attendees, Kavya named Anjali, Drishti, Suchi, Vihaan, Nikhil, Jay, Mayank, and Arnav. Sudden energy sparked after reading the name I wanted on the list. I dashed to my room and took a few clothes from the closet. I finally settled on a peach-coloured top and dark blue jeans.

Kavya and I reached the venue on time, as did all the other girls. We all started gossiping the moment we met, waiting for the boys. Anjali called one of the boys to inquire about their whereabouts. All the boys arrived after a while, except for Arnav. Kavya, as if reading my mind, asked about him.

'He is not picking up my calls,' Vihaan said, entering the restaurant. 'Guess he isn't coming.'

The dining hall was alive with our voices only. I kept looking at the entrance in hopes of seeing him until the food arrived. I listened to everyone's story about their college and its culture. I wonder sometimes, *do the boys know my name? I am not even a member of the school WhatsApp group. Am I supposed to be here in that case?*

'Hiya, how is the food?' Vihaan, sitting in front of me, cheerily questioned.

I looked up suddenly. 'Very good. The *paneer chilli* is delicious.'

'The best in town,' he added. 'You know, you're also allowed to speak. Don't be so quiet.'

I responded with a fake grin. From inside, I had drowned myself in embarrassment. *It was a bad idea to come and join these people. I could have gone for a night walk with my Doodle.* The only good thought that came out of my mind was that *Vihaan knew my name.*

I came back home after attending the boring dinner. How I imagined my dinner and how differently it turned out. I had high hopes for making new memories to cherish, but it wasn't an exciting day. *What could have gone wrong with him?*

Kavya sent me pictures of the dinner party. Even though I wanted to and despite her insistence, I refused to join the school's WhatsApp group. That's the thing about Introverts, they want to be invited but are too shy to go. They need pampering and caring like an indoor plant.

Doodle followed me from the kitchen to my room. I recalled about the pending assignments as I saw my backpack. The deadline to submit it was two days away. The assignment were of the structural subject, the toughest one. The never-ending step-by-step calculations are tricky and lengthy. My college friend, Rahul, has been a clever student in that particular subject and he always let me copy his assignments. His future goal is to achieve a master's degree in structural engineering, and mine is to finish a bachelor's first and then decide.

I set up the table with assignment papers, my book, Indian Standard Codes, some stationary materials and began to solve. Till the fourth step, I solved the sum, but then an unfamiliar and unsuitable number started appearing magically. I couldn't solve the mystery. I had only one hope. I dropped a message to Rahul. Soon, he sent me pictures of his assignment. I got scared by the amount of work. To copy that much work, I needed energy. I went to the kitchen and made sure to take out the dish without making a sound, but it clattered. Doodle came snooping in the kitchen following me.

'You're hungry?' I asked softly. Doodle agreed with a puppy-like intonation. I poured some pedigree into one bowl and filled my bowl with popcorn. When I finished writing, it was one in the clock. My spine and neck were screaming for rest.

Arnav

'Hey, you should've taken the flyover. I'll miss my train because of you,' I shouted at the rickshaw driver. 'Slow down this music, please. It's annoying,' I yelled again, losing my cool. He ignored my pleas and continued repeating song lines. His behaviour infuriated me. I ordered him to halt the rickshaw, paid half the fee, and hired another one. He was fast enough to drop me at the station.

I ran with the speed of top gear, putting all the braking systems apart, colliding with every third person from the rickshaw stand to platform number two of Surat railway station, just to see how my train looks while running on the rail track. The next train was after one hour. My phone was dead. I realised after checking my backpack that I had forgotten to pack the charger. Sitting in the waiting room, watching people around me, I blamed the rickshaw driver for his pathetic driving skills. But I was angrier with my lecturer for extending the lecture hours without our permission.

I was exhausted by the time I reached home. My mother served hot masala tea with snacks. I was narrating my day when the doorbell rang.

'That must be your father,' my mother said. I rushed to open the main door. Cookie, my four-month-old black and tan German shepherd, leaped on me. All my stress vanished the moment I wrapped my arms around her. The excitement of meeting me after several days was bouncing in her. The happiness that she has brought into my life is unbeatable. She stole my entire heart the moment I met her for the first time when me and my parents decided to have a dog.

After dinner, I laid on the bed. I suddenly remembered that I had a gathering to attend. It was completely gone from my thoughts. I hastily looked for a charger to charge my phone. When it came to life, messages kept dropping like indiscriminate fire. There were four hundred messages, eight missed calls, news notifications, and company messages.

On the chat group, my college friends were berating our lecturer for ruining our day. I chuckled aloud at a few of the funny texts, which caused inconvenience to Cookie's sleep. She expressed her disdain from her tiny bed on the floor. While scrolling, I saw the group name *'Where are you, Arnav?'* with an angry emoji. I read all the messages and downloaded photographs of the dinner party, which I missed because of my stupid dead phone, my cruel professor, and that idiot rickshaw driver.

Remove Arnav from this group.

He is the most absent guy… did the same act in the Diwali reunion.

I'm telling you he is none of us now.

He was the one urging to plan a get together since last Diwali and choose his college friends… we are no one now.

I read the messages in which all my friends were rebuking me online.

Guys I am really very extremely sorry. I had a very bad day. I sent the text. It wasn't easy convincing them to forgive me, but I made it possible.

I checked the pictures and saw everyone with one more girl, Hiya, who wasn't part of the school group. At first, I didn't recognise her. She was my schoolmate and to whom everyone used to call the silent and obedient girl. I fell into the trap of teenage attraction for her during school time for a while but came out of it once I decided on a serious career goal to join the list of prominent architects in my country.

Being a student of architecture, it's hard to maintain a good relationship between sleep and studies. Either you can complete your sleep or your drawings. My favourite place to hang out is the stationery shop, where I can buy useless things for my model. But I know that I chose the correct path for me. The wonderful and astonishing combination of art and engineering reflects how excellent this field is.

Me and three other classmates had taken a flat on rent as travelling daily from another city was tough. However, I try to visit my hometown, Navsari, every possible weekend so that I can spend quality time with my family. Whenever I come, I never miss a chance to see my school buddies. Vihaan is my closest friend and has a special place in my heart. He is my future civil engineer. We both got our admission in different city apart from our hometown but for him it's possible to travel daily from one city to other.

The atmosphere was wonderful outside. It wasn't raining but the thunder was rumbling. As a token of an apology I planned a meeting with all the boys at the Phoenix Cafe. I got some serious fist punches from all of them for my absence at the party.

'Look, our future architect has finally found some time for his not so important friends,' Nikhil taunted.

'Will you stop being sarcastic?' I said without any expression.

'Did you break up with your pencil and paper?' Mayank poked next.

'You deserve it,' Jay said and we all took our seats.

Vihaan grabbed my neck and pushed me down. 'Couldn't you just inform me before?' He said increasing his hand pressure.

Nikhil raised his five fingers in the air as a sign of *five filtered coffees*. The waiter nodded with a smile and raised his thumb. We got to hear from Jay that our chemistry teacher was retiring from her duties and the farewell function was scheduled for August 15, after the flag hoisting ceremony. Vihaan excitedly suggested that we attend the function and do something for our teacher. Everyone acknowledged his idea. The waiter served us coffee. He was happy to see us after a long time.

'Now that you've found me, will you please change the name of the group?' I said, showing Vihaan my phone. While peering at the screen, Vihaan's eyes rolled away.

'That's Hiya, right?' He asked, confused. I turned my face to see. I couldn't see her as she turned around. She walked near the pastry and cake section, a few feet away from us.

'Is that her dog? That's a white retriever,' I said, amazed. 'I never knew she had a dog!' I said, watching her dog trying to climb on the glass shelf.

'No, Doodle. Stay away,' she said, handling the leash. There I caught a glimpse of her. She collected her order and moved out.

'She is looking pretty, isn't she?' Vihaan said, staring at her. All the four faces with eight eyes, including mine, looked abruptly at Vihaan.

'Just giving a compliment,' Vihaan stated, sipping coffee.

'What's your girlfriend doing, Arnav?' Nikhil asked.

'She is enjoying her life and growing so fast,' I said with excitement. 'Do they allow pets in here? I could have brought her here.'

'Whoa! Never ever think of that. You know that I am afraid of dogs,' Vihaan declared.

'That's your problem not mine,' I laughed. We all laughed.

Hiya

'Ma, I am leaving for college,' I shouted, tying the strings of my shoes. 'See you soon, Doodoo,' I scrubbed Doodle's head. He never felt good seeing me leaving the house. I rushed to catch the college bus from the society entrance.

I saw Rahul, present in the class before me. I thanked him for his help. 'I've got some horrifying news for you,' he said, smiling. 'I overheard our professor about a surprise test for structure soon,' he whispered in my ear. That shocked me, indeed.

Rahul has been a brilliant student, topper of the class, and good friend of mine since our second year of college. Apart from studies, He has been a good cricket player. In last year's sports festival, his amazing batting helped us win the victory cup. I've seen him as an honest person who doesn't care about ranks, helps everyone who comes with a query.

When the last bell rang, it started raining. *Does the rain follow the college schedules too, or does it follow my schedule?* Whenever I have to go somewhere, with all due respect, the rain never misses its chance to greet me with its water drops. I love watching the rain, sipping a hot cup of tea, and sitting on my balcony, but getting wet is an awful experience, especially when going out for important work.

The raincoats are useless in heavy rain. *The water will find its way.* What truthful words! It's advisable to choose a mode of transportation with a roof over your head, and so I use college buses in the monsoon months. I rushed towards my bus as I saw the familiar number plate to reserve my seat.

Arnav

I was back to my routine with the bunch of cardboard, papers, drawing sheets, pens, and colours. In the studio, my hunt for a pen, pencil, eraser, and glue is an unending process. All my equipment mysteriously goes missing, and other people's stationary goes missing because of me. That's how I play fair games. It was a hectic day. When I came back to my flat, I was completely exhausted. I checked my phone, lying on the bed. There was a message from Vihaan on the school chat group.

Hola, guys and girls. Can someone share Hiya's number? She isn't in the group.

Kavya shared the number and Vihaan, the group admin, added her. Everyone welcomed her. Later, Vihaan announced our chemistry teacher's farewell function. The girls also showed their interest in attending the function. Vihaan gave everyone the responsibility of coming up with an idea for a farewell present for our teacher.

My chat box kept filling with messages. Ideas kept coming from my friends. I fell asleep unknowingly, and when I woke up, it was already 7:45 a.m. I reached college before the history of architecture lecture started. It would have created a problem for me otherwise. My professor honestly doesn't know how to teach at all. Just for the sake of attendance, I witnessed his boring methods of teaching.

I read the pending messages in his lecture. Anjali was completely out of her mind, who suggested gifting a golden chain. *What does she think we are? Millionaires?* Suchi proposed a customised coffee mug and pen. Mayank indicated a digital gift card. Nikhil's idea sounded good to me. A wooden frame with a thank-you note and a flower bouquet. At the end of the day, his idea got elected with the most votes.

My college may not have the best teachers in the world, but the canteen at my college is the world's best. Every dish is delicious at an affordable price. When you live in a city like Surat, famous for its tasty and spicy food, the city won't let you sleep with an empty stomach. You'll find tastes from all over the world on the streets of Surat, as well as the foodies of the city. *Locho* is life here. *Fafda and jalebi* are an unbeatable combination. The most loved sweet of the city, coated with ghee is the gratifying *Ghari,* the well-known cold drink of the city with a tagline *apna desh, apna drink, Sosyo,* and the list goes on and on.

The people of this city have the courage to spend a big amount of money on food in one day. A man's way to win his heart goes through his stomach, and this city has enough to offer that can win your heart every day, not just for men but for women, children, and people of all ages. Maintaining your health and weight is a little difficult here.

* * *

I am planning to join AutoCAD classes. You wanted to learn some software too, right?

I read Vihaan's text message. I had learned AutoCAD a long time ago, but I had plans to learn another software to amplify my skills. When Vihaan asked me, I made up my mind to join him.

Hiya

July 26, 2015.

Dear Doodle,

I am blessed to have you in my life. Though you are just an animal, you understand all my moods very well. You are the perfect boyfriend and the one whose world revolves around me, the one who gets happy when I am happy, the one who gets sad when I am sad, and the one who loves to follow me. To live without you is unimaginable. You're the biggest joy of my life.

Although you have a very short lifespan, you spend half the time waiting for me to come from college or anywhere. No humans can do that, or I can say no humans have time to wait for someone so eagerly except my mother, who waits for my father to come home from work. Whenever the clock ticks past 7 in the evening, she start counting minutes.

The day when I held you for the first time in my hands was the happiest moment of my life. It was a dream come true. I'll never forget that day when I saw you sitting on my bed and my parents waiting for me to open my eyes and record the reaction of their best surprise. You matter more to me than anything.

* * *

When the bell rang, the professor showed up with a bunch of papers in hand. I guessed about it and looked at Rahul. Next minute, the professor announced the test. Horror echoed in the classroom. Everyone started murmuring with a petrified face.

'Only two students per bench and no cheating,' he declared and distributed test papers.

Rahul started solving the structural mysteries the minute he got the paper. I am an average student when it comes to structural analysis. But somehow, I managed to reach the end and complete the sum. All my gratitude goes to Indian Standard Codes for showing me the path. I tried to look at Rahul's answer sheets, but he was turning pages briskly and his fingers were dancing on the calculator. The speed at which his pen was moving raised my curiosity as to whether he knew the questions as well!

There was a pin-drop silence in the class. We were in the middle of a test when a message beeped on someone's phone. The professor expressed his anger and asked to submit the phone. One boy stood up and said '*Results of the 4th semester are out!*' Anxiety began whispering within the class.

'SILENCE!' Our professor roared and tapped the duster on the table. 'The result isn't running anywhere. Complete the test first.'

A few students, including Rahul, started writing like nothing happened. In my case, staring at the buffering circle while waiting for the result screen to show up is more threatening than watching the result. I tried hard to concentrate.

'Stop writing and submit your answer sheets,' the professor declared when the bell rang.

The minute he left the classroom with answer sheets, everyone pulled out their phones to see the results. *Have you got the result? Is your website open? Is it working? How many points did you get? You got any backlog?* Anxious questions from all directions were hitting my ears like stones. *Show me the sentence painted in green, please.* Biting my nails, I kept repeating the lines peering at my phone.

'Yes! It's 8.9.' Rahul jumped with excitement. One by one, everyone was declaring their results, and mine was still stuck somewhere. The more everyone was screaming their results, the faster my heartbeats were running. At last, my eyes were pleased to read the green lines. *Congratulations!! You have passed this exam.* I got 7.9, which was one point behind Rahul's.

'I was expecting more than 9 this time,' Rahul expressed his agony.

I wondered why Rahul was complaining about not getting number 9. With or without a difference in his points, he still managed to top, just like in the previous semester. He should not be the one worrying about a 0.1 thing, but I should because my friend, Priya, got a perfect 8. She consoled me when I complained about my points. My parents were happy to know my results. For the rest of the day, stupid 0.1 occupied my mind. Overthinking is one of my qualities or my inbuilt hobby, I can say!

When I reached home, all my worries flew away as I saw my fur-ball running towards me. Holding up his two paws, we danced. My father brought ice cream for the celebration.

One of our seniors was asking me if anyone is interested in learning AutoCAD. He is looking for more people. I read Priya's message in the group. I refused, as I was thinking of learning it in my final year.

Later that night, I was scrolling through my WhatsApp to see everyone's profile picture. My eyes stuck on the newest added contact number, Arnav's picture. I saw a picture of him with his dog, a baby German shepherd. I never knew that there was a common link between us. I never knew that he has an affection for dogs just like me! My inner soul couldn't control its excitements. The German shepherd is a cool breed but dangerous, too. *My Doodle is the best!*

Arnav

I decided to become an architect after clearing my 10th. My keenness to observe the details, textures, and carvings of any ancient structure has encouraged me. Despite the amount of pressure this field holds, I found it interesting. The more I've involved myself in this field year after year, the more I've become eager to learn new things. I promised myself to put anything at stake to make my dream come true.

There are times when I miss my Cookie. I wanted to bring her with me. Then I imagined myself coming to my flat from college and see all my hard work chewed and torn by her in my absence. So, I dropped the idea. On the contrary, I was so influenced by Hiya's retriever. She had a picture of her dog in her WhatsApp, just like me! I wanted to ask her about her dog, and other qualities, how she takes care. I searched her Instagram profile and sent the request.

My flat-mate knocked on the door. 'The cook isn't coming today. Let's go out for dinner,' he said.

'I have only 500 rupees left in my pocket. How will I survive?'

'Same as you, man but no other option,' he answered.

My friend had brought his two-wheeler from home, so there was no problem with spending hundreds on rickshaw rent every month. After having a masala dosa, we stopped for a glass of lemon soda without caring for the countable money left in our pockets. A glass of ten-rupee soda made no difference.

Just when I reached back, I got a call from my mother. *What are you doing, beta? Have you eaten? Why was the cook on leave? Are you coming this weekend?* She raised a new question at the end of my every answer. Sometimes I get irritated, but I like talking about my day with her. She gave me all the details of her day. I listened to it without any tantrums, but there comes a time when I pretend to listen.

Hiya

How do you feel when you want something to happen and it happens automatically? There is no point in keeping your social media account secret when the purpose is to show the world how you live or enjoy life, and what you eat. I don't carry any hard-core secrets behind that one button, but being a private person, I like to keep it that way. I checked my notification and saw the Instagram request from an account named _arnav_17.

I scrolled to the end of his profile. It had a lot of architectural stuff and eye-catching photography. I intentionally accepted the request after half an hour. It raised my follower count to 100. Arnav had more than 500 followers. I took a step forward and sent him a request on Facebook. He approved it in five minutes. *Was he waiting for my move?* The silent, nonverbal communication between us was so satisfying to me.

It felt like the rain had settled in Navsari since the first day of August. The sun wasn't in the mood to come out and shine. People like my father, who like to join their hands daily to the rising sun, were not lucky enough to do it. He would pray to the black and white clouds, then would complain about being unable to see the sun. My father's daily routine includes chanting several shlokas for half an hour. No one can dare speak a word whenever he prays, not even Doodle!

* * *

Dear Doodle,

August 5, 2015,

Writing your feelings on paper is like telling someone something you're unable to say. It helps you lighten your heart. It is soothing and relaxing. I made writing a habit because thirty, forty, or fifty years from today, I might not remember what happened on certain days, but this diary will. It will save all the happy, sad, funny, and silly moments of my life. So, keeping a diary is like having a backup of the past life, or, in other words, I can say it's a time travel machine to revisit the best time of the life at any time. It will work as an escape when I'll become the grumpy old lady, searching for a reason to live life without you!

There are no movements on the school WhatsApp group, and I wonder if the farewell got spoiled because of the rain. I thought to ask Kavya, but the over-thinker in me discouraged me by advising that it isn't a good idea. If there is no plan, then I can give the salute to the flag and sing the national anthem in my college on August 15.

The rain vanished the next day and the sun was gleaming happily in the sky. My father couldn't stop praising the glorious sun god. From newly born tiny baby leaves to enormous leaves breathed the fresh sunlight after numerous days. Hidden beneath the mighty noise of rain, all the bird's morning melodies came to life once again. Standing in the balcony of my room, I scrutinised nature. The trees in my society are home to a wide range of birds. I spend hours with my camera for the perfect photographer's click.

In college, during break time, I got the notification of *'anyone here?'* from Vihaan on the chat group. I waited for someone to reply and Anjali texted *'I am here'* One by one everyone commented on their presence including me.

August 15th & sharp 7:45 in the morning at school. Be there everyone.

The plan was finally executed and all conquered.

In the canteen, Rahul discussed his plans to attempt the GATE exams for post-graduation. He had joined a coaching class for that. I felt pity on myself, observing his efforts. He had already learned AutoCAD in the previous year, and now he was taking steps ahead for his future. Following his dedication, I changed my mind and decided to sign up for software learning classes.

Vihaan

I cut the alarm for the third time without looking at the phone. A constant, loud thudding on the door woke me up.

'Don't you want to go to school for the flag-hoisting ceremony?' I heard my mother saying from behind the closed door. She rushed back to the kitchen. My eyes widened when I saw 6:50 on the clock.

'Can you please iron my shirt, Risha? I am very late.' I requested my sister when I saw her passing from my room.

'And why on earth would I do that?' She stopped and said.

I apologised to her for eating her pizza on previous night but she didn't bother to consider. I tried one more time by assuring to get one more pizza of her choice, but that also didn't work. She showed attitude, mocked my helplessness and turned away.

'You know what, I don't need your help,' I shouted on her back. 'And yes, I'll eat from your plate. Stop me if you can.' I shouted more loudly.

'You're getting late, Vihaan,' I heard her reply.

I sought my mother's help, but she denied it too, saying she was busy with kitchen work. *It is a curse to be the youngest in this family. I help everyone, but no one's there for me.* I complained to myself.

Be ready by 7:30. I texted Arnav, and I hurried to get ready.

My neatly pressed white shirt, with a hard-to-find wrinkle on it, was placed on the bed as I stepped out of the bathroom.

'One farmhouse cheese burst and garlic breadsticks with cheese dip.' I heard Risha, standing at the door, commanding me. 'You owe me that. Okay?'

'I'll have a slice from it for sure,' I said with a broad smile and embraced her.

'Aren't you getting late?' She said in a muffled voice. Despite the three-year age gap, I exceeded her height long ago with a five-inch difference.

The clock showed 7:10. I hastily put on my clothes, combed my hair, sprayed perfume, and was ready to leave. My mother gave me a mug full of milk with extra Bournvita.

'Happy Independence Day, ma,' I greeted her and kissed her cheek. I saw my father coming in from jogging.

'Daddy, Can I take your car please?' I asked, crossed my fingers in the hope of *yes*.

'No,' he said sharply, picking up the newspaper.

'Please, please, I promise I'll handle it with care.' I requested.

He gave me a sharper look. I was standing in front of him with a face saying *I really want to drive that car.*

'Alright, but the speed limit is 50 max.' I don't know what melted his mind but I was super happy.

'I'll drive at 40. Thank you.' I excitedly rushed to grab the key.

'Daddy! That's totally not fair,' my sister yelled. 'You never let me drive your car!' She said, complaining. I looked at her angrily for giving my father a chance to reconsider his decision.

'Fine. Next time, you can take it. Happy?' He said and headed towards the garden to read the newspaper in a natural environment while sipping hot tea.

'Happy Independence Day, Sis!' I teased her to make her realise I finally got the freedom to drive the car and to sprinkle salt on her wound, and I showed her the car key. The jealousy was clearly visible on her face.

I informed Arnav and placed the farewell present on the back seat. I put on my glasses, pressed the start button, and the engine roared. I tightened my grip on the steering wheel and pushed the accelerator. The dream of driving my father's Mercedes finally came true. I reached Arnav's place in ten minutes. I wanted to see his expressions live and kept it a secret. I pressed down on the window button and blew the horn. Arnav looked at me with open mouth.

'Beauty and the Beast!' Arnav roared with excitement, the moment he saw me. 'You did it, Man! You did it,' he said loudly.

'Hop on,' I said, flashing my smile.

'I'll be taking the driver's seat next,' he said, buckling the seat belt.

The whole town was covered in saffron, white, and green. On our way, we saw many people with tri-colour in their hands, waving proudly on their bikes.

'Lovely morning! Isn't it?' Arnav said.

'Yeah, that's true,' I said, indicating the left signal, took a turn, drove inside the gate, and stopped at the place where me and all my friends met for the first time many years ago, 'B. S. High School'.

Hiya

I glanced up at the sky to see if there was any chance of rain while I waited for Kavya. The sky looked clear, with scattered white clouds. I was swinging on the wooden swing. Doodle had laid himself on the floor comfortably near the swing. My mother shouted from the kitchen and advised my father, who was busy reading each and every line of the newspaper, to drink his tea before it turns cold. I had put on my sky-blue kurta for the occasion.

Doodle, the moment he saw an unknown rider near the gate of his home, barked loudly. Kavya couldn't dare to trespass the gate and asked me to take the seat. I informed my mother before leaving.

We saw students buying the flag from the vendors standing outside the school gate and took it for ourselves. Other girls joined us too. Without wasting time, we entered school territory, and a flashback of memories greeted me. All the scooters and bicycles were parked at the same place where we used to park once. The trees and plants were very well maintained. There were few new plantations of the trees I saw. I noticed that the walls of the schools were repainted wheat brown and the borders were painted coffee brown. It felt so good walking on the school ground again where our tiny footsteps walked once.

I saw teachers gathering near the stage where the flag-hoisting ceremony happens every year. The students were rushing to take their place. It was all so noisy until, as usual, our PT teacher came down from the stage blowing a whistle and gesturing everyone to make proper lines and stand with discipline. Watching the students giggle and gossip while standing in line reminded us of our carefree days.

The music teacher and a few students seemed busy practising at the last minute. All the boys except Vihaan and Arnav had already come. I had no expectations for Arnav to come and make my day but Nikhil mentioned that they both were coming together. *I'll finally get to see him.*

We saw a glossy white car enter through the gate. The eye-catching car, considering its logo of a three-pointed star, was a Mercedes. The car caught our attention, including that of teachers standing near us. I thought it was a guest invited by the school, but I was wrong. I saw two young boys in the car, wearing sunglasses. I couldn't recognise them due to the reflection of the tree branches on the wind shield.

The white light shut as the engine stopped, and the next second, the doors were opened. The boys were none other than Arnav and Vihaan. I was stupefied. Walking towards us, they met the physics teacher in the midst. Arnav and Vihaan stopped to greet him. Both of them touched the teacher's feet and talked for a while, maybe about studies.

While peering at them, I wondered that both the boys in white shirts looked like twin brothers. The only difference between them was the colour of their jeans. Their skin was glowing in the warm sunlight. I was not wrong at all about my immature feelings towards Arnav during school time. Seeing him after a very long time, I found it hard to find a way out of these thoughts. However, Vihaan was also giving a tough competition in his bright white shirt. He seemed as good as Arnav. I wondered how I never recognised him and completely ignored him during school.

It was the 69th Independence Day of India, and the whole country was celebrating it with great enthusiasm. The honour of hoisting the flag was given to our chemistry teacher. As she pulled the string, the flag got untied, swung proudly in the air, and the flower petals stuffed inside touched the ground. Everyone clapped, and on the command of the PT teacher, we saluted the flag.

The principal began her speech. In her fifteen-minute speech, she remembered all the great leaders, freedom fighters, and martyred soldiers and stated the progress of the school, which bored all students. In the end, she mentioned the chemistry teacher's contribution towards school and gave her a flower bouquet with a present wrapped in shiny paper.

As a part of the celebrations, our music teacher and her students came first to sing. Primary and secondary school students sang patriotic songs in groups, with dance performances included. After an hour, the function ended with the national anthem.

When the PT teacher announced that students could head back to their homes, the finely classified rows of students dispersed like pearls from a broken necklace. We, the former students, made our way through the flood of rushing students and successfully managed to meet our teacher. As a sign of being good students, we all touched her feet one by one. She burst into tears upon accepting the bouquet and the gift. She was overwhelmed and couldn't stop praising us. She recalled how all the boys used to annoy her so much in the chemistry lab.

We visited the classroom of the 12th standard, where we spent the never-to-be-forgotten last year of school life. It was an extreme honour to be the seniors in the entire school. The smell of the classroom made me nostalgic. The blackboard, table, chair, and benches were in the same place.

'I found it,' Nikhil shouted from the last bench. 'I can't believe it is still here,' he said gleefully. All the boys gathered near him.

'*Vihaan, Arnav, and Nikhil were here. Year 2013.*' Mayank read the line crafted by Vihaan. The classroom breathed in the old aroma again with the more mature sound of its former students.

The topics for boys were endless. The more time we spent there, the more and more old stories popped up. We were so busy revisiting the past that we completely forgot to look at the present. More than half an hour had passed when the peon came to lock the door. The school ground was empty when we came out. Kavya's phone rang, and she walked away to answer the call.

Standing with the other girls, I caught a glimpse of Arnav, posing with both hands in his jeans pocket. Vihaan, standing in front of him, was clicking pictures. They reversed their roles later, and Arnav took pictures of Vihaan. I changed my sight briskly when Kavya came and informed me that she had to go and pick up her aunt from the railway station.

'I'll take a rickshaw from here, don't worry,' I said. She apologised to me.

'Sorry and worry for what?' Vihaan interrupted. 'Any trouble?' He added. Kavya repeated her story.

'We'll drop Hiya,' Vihaan said. I looked at him abruptly. 'Trust me, I am always in search of a reason to drive a car.'

'I've already booked the driver's seat,' Arnav, who was checking the photos in his phone, said to Vihaan.

Kavya thanked Vihaan before leaving.

'I think we should leave before the gatekeeper locks us in the school,' Vihaan insisted to everyone. 'Come on, lead us the way, Hiya.' He walked to his car.

I obeyed the footsteps of Vihaan and Arnav. *Will I have to talk? What will I say? Can I just run away? I believe that both boys are very smart and sensible, but no, I don't want to go. I should have brought my scooter. I shouldn't have come. I should have gone to the college function. But I won't get this chance for a fancy car ride with Arnav again. I just wish to reach home soon.*

The interior of the car looked attractive with its black and white leather cover. The three-pointed star logo fixed in the centre of the steering wheel looked so luxurious. The engine rumbled as Arnav hit the start button. The cool air circulated in the car within a few seconds.

'I can't believe I am finally driving this,' Arnav said, moving his fingers over the steering wheel.

'It is so smooth man! I can ride all day,' Vihaan said. 'You comfortable, Hiya?' He asked, turning his face to me.

'Yes… I am fine,' I, who was peeking outside the window, turned my face all of a sudden.

'I hope you're not thinking that we'll kidnap you!' Vihaan said and laughed.

'No…' I joined his fake laugh.

Arnav clicked on the accelerator, and the wheels began spinning.

'Arnii.. you didn't reply to me on your software learning programme,' Vihaan said to Arnav.

'Revit. I am planning to learn. Have you got the details about the class here?'

'Yes, the more students I bring, the more discount in fees we'll get.'

'Straight?' Arnav asked.

'What?' Baffled, Vihaan looked at Arnav.

'Hiya?' Arnav asked, looking at me from the rearview mirror. I was busy reading messages.

'Yes. straight ahead and then left,' I replied quickly. That was the first time I heard my name from Arnav. I put my phone aside to concentrate on the road.

'We are heading towards LK Road. We can have a plate of *Locho*. What do you say?' Vihaan suggested it and turned to me. 'Are you okay with the idea, Hiya? It's on me,' he said showing excitement.

'Say yes, Hiya, you'll never get this chance again. I'm still waiting for my treat for his last birthday,' Arnav lamented, looking at the rearview mirror. Our eyes met this time.

'Okay!' I agreed. I couldn't explain to them that I already had my breakfast and my mother would have prepared lunch by now.

The car stopped near one mini food truck with a board named '*Surti Locho*' on top. I came out of the car and saw my phone that I left inside it.

'My... My phone is inside,' I stopped Arnav, who was walking ahead.

He unlocked the car and opened the door for me. Vihaan stood in the queue to bring the order. I and Arnav waited for Vihaan. *What should I talk about, and how? You've got such a good chance, Hiya. Talk to him.* I was talking with Arnav in my mind without caring about his presence in the present.

'What are you studying right now?' Arnav asked, instead of standing there silently pretending to observe the world.

'Engineering... civil engineering.' The inner voice was laughing at me for my paralysed behaviour.

'That's good. I am studying Architecture,' he said quickly.

Vihaan brought the plates of *locho* for us.

'Vihaan is looking for people who want to learn AutoCAD. If you're interested, you can join,' Arnav said.

'Never knew that you're into engineering,' Vihaan replied. 'I am looking for students, right now it's just Arnav and me,' Vihaan said, putting bites, one after another in his mouth.

This could be your chance Hiya to know Arnav more. Opportunity is knocking your door. Don't let it go. Say yes and this could be a new turning in your life. In two minutes, I made the decision to join them.

'Actually, I was already planning to join.'

'Great! I am going to confirm my admission next week. You can invite your classmates as well.'

I nodded. He gave me details regarding the academy. Being a slow eater, I still had 4-5 bites left on the plate. Arnav, who had already finished, took a bite from my plate. 'With cheese is much better,' Arnav declared.

* * *

I expressed my gratitude, getting out of the car, for dropping me home.

'It's my turn to drive,' Vihaan said.

The moment Vihaan saw my Doodle rushing towards the car from the half-opened gate, he immediately pulled out Arnav and took the driver's seat, closing the door behind him. Arnav didn't panic.

'That's yours?' Arnav asked when Doodle was showering his affection on me.

'Yeah, you can call him Doodle,' I said.

'I've got a baby German Shepherd, Cookie,' Arnav said excitedly. 'Hey buddy,' he said, rubbing Doodle's forehead.

'Doodle love free massages.' I said, watching Arnav getting comfortable with my dog.

'Can we go now?' Vihaan asked.

'Vihaan is so afraid of dogs,' Arnav grinned and sat back in the car.

Arnav

'That was the healthiest and most energetic retriever I've ever seen,' I told Vihaan.

'Dog lover, she is as crazy as you!' Vihaan mocked.

Vihaan wanted to leave after dropping me but I dragged him out of his car and took him to my home.

'Ma will be happy to see you,' I said. The lift stopped on the fifth floor. When I rang the doorbell, Vihaan suddenly took his steps back and stood close to the stairs. His sudden movement mystified me, and at the same moment I realised his fear of dogs. Looking at his scared face, I couldn't control my laughter.

'Hold your dog first. I don't want to die,' Vihaan said. He was all set to use the stairs in case Cookie decided to jump on him first. He got more scared as he heard Cookie barking. I told my mother to lock Cookie in the room and then open the door.

'The road's been cleared. You may walk in,' I said. 'Watching your face is really funny, Vihaan,' I released my laugh again.

'Stop teasing him,' ma said to me. Vihaan stepped forward and embraced her.

'How are you?' Vihaan asked.

'Very good and you?' She said and took his face in her palms.

'I am all good.'

Vihaan's mother and my mother were studying together in college days and they passed on their bond of friendship in me and Vihaan. She went to the kitchen. We both followed in her footsteps. Vihaan pulled out the coldest water bottle from the refrigerator. I passed the steel glass to him and took the bottle. I gulped water directly from it. Vihaan saw my mother making his most-loved *puranpoli* and demanded one to eat. My mother asked us to take a seat at the dining table to eat. I brought the plates and ma served us.

'Have you eaten?' I asked ma.

'I am waiting for your father to come,' she said. 'Did he forget his way? What is taking so long? Let me call him,' she said, and went in search of her phone.

'It's delicious!' Vihaan praised goodness with every bite.

Our chit-chat continued at the table till we finished eating. After gulping water, we burped together and looked at each other. When ma came back, she forgot to close the bedroom door. Cookie took no time to come out. Vihaan, who was putting the chair back in place, saw Cookie.

'Arniii…' He rushed to the other end of the table. 'Hold your dog!' He shouted. Cookie gained speed as she sensed a stranger in her house, barking loudly. I clutched her collar in the middle while she was aiming for Vihaan.

'Easy girl. He is family. Do not hurt him. Okay?' I tightened my grip as she was trying hard to release herself. I gestured to Vihaan to relax. I took Cookie to my room and closed the door. Vihaan was preparing to leave when I came back to the living room. My mother urged Vihaan to spend more time with her, but Vihaan's father wanted the car.

I took Cookie for a walk after a while. 'Let's see who runs faster, baby!' I gave her a competitive look and ran, holding the leash in my hand. Once I let her run without a leash, she started chasing other dogs roaming in the streets. After running a few hundred metres, I started panting, but she was full of energy.

'You are gro… growing so fast… so fast,' I said, still breathless. 'Better we walk… okay!'

* * *

The next day, the boys meet-up was fixed at the Phoenix Cafe. We saw Hiya and Kavya sitting on the table where we usually sit.

'Those are our seats, girls,' Vihaan said. 'It is permanently reserved for us, don't you know?' He teased them.

'Oh, really!' Kavya replied with a smile. 'Then you might want to join us. Do you?'

'Nah. I am just kidding. Have fun.' Vihaan took the cherry off the top of Kavya's black forest pastry.

Though it was Sunday, the cafe was half empty. We took a table next to the girls. I exchanged my gaze with Hiya multiple times. She changed her sight briskly, as if I caught her staring at me. The waiter presented filtered coffee to us.

'Mayank, Nikhil, I wanted to ask you guys something?' Vihaan spoke.

'Wait, is it about asking to join AutoCAD class?' I stopped Vihaan in the middle.

'Yup,' Vihaan replied with a wide smile.

'Oh god!' I said it irritably. 'Will you stop selling tickets for AutoCAD? It has nothing to do with what they study,' I said, pointing my hands at Nikhil and Mayank. I saw Hiya and Kavya giggling and enjoying the scene. Vihaan kept mum for a while.

'Are you two alone, or are the other girls going to join you?' Vihaan asked the girls. He was sitting close to them.

'It's just me and Hiya today,' Kavya replied. 'By the way, thanks for dropping Hiya home.'

'It's my duty.' Vihaan smiled.

I couldn't decide whether he was part of our group or theirs because half of the time his head was turned towards the girls. We all came out of the cafe together. Hiya and Kavya faded away on their scooters. Sitting on the bench of

LK ground, we boys continued our discussions of cricket and politics and Bollywood and so on till the shades of evening sky got darker.

* * *

My whole week was busy with lots of work. My sleeping and eating times were badly messed up. Though Friday was relaxing compared to other days, at least I ate dinner on time. I buried myself in the beanbag, opened my phone, and began scrolling. I refreshed the feed, and the first picture that showed up on my screen was a dog, Hiya's retriever, sitting in the garden in between the long grass, smiling. The combination of green grass with tiny fresh water droplets on it and the white dog sitting in the centre was so beautiful. The tiny, multi-coloured wild flowers were giving a cherry on top look to the photograph. I double-tapped to like the photo. I fell in love with her dog the moment I brushed my fingers on its forehead.

Should I ask whether she has decided to join the class? But I'll get to know it anyway. I can at least ask just to start a conversation. Maybe she'll let me play with her Doodle again. The negative and positive sides of my mind were busy creating chaos for me. At last, I finally decided to ask. It took a lot of time for me to type a simple *hi*. She replied back in two minutes. She was coming on Sunday!

* * *

There was no sign of Vihaan when I reached 'The Art Academy'. I waited for him and dialled his number multiple times but no response I received from him.

'Where were you, man?' I growled as he showed himself. I was sure he would've fallen asleep, and I was right.

A few more students that Vihaan managed to gather from his college, came after him. Hiya was still missing. Vihaan advised me to call her. 'Don't you have your phone?' I whined.

'It's dead. I forgot to charge.'

'You idiot useless son of a millionaire!' I sighed heavily, pulling my phone from my pocket.

'There she is.' Vihaan spotted her crossing the road on her scooter. She greeted us warmly. We all fit ourselves in one lift.

'Do not leave any doubt in your mind. Feel free to ask whatever you want to,' Vihaan whispered before pushing the door inside.

The owner of the academy welcomed us and led us to his cabin. He politely began spreading words about his academy and their services. He explained everything in detail. In the end, he asked us about our doubts. My software was different from others, so I waited for my turn.

I had to make things clear about my uncertainty about attending the classes as I lived in a different city. He said *there is no register that counts your presence.* He gave us a good deduction in fees, thanks to Vihaan, who was promoting their academy free of charge. Hours from four to six in the evening were finalised for Saturday and Sunday. We all booked our seats with a token amount of a thousand rupees.

'You must be the happiest person on the Earth right now, aren't you?' I told Vihaan after coming out.

'Well, you can say that,' Vihaan replied, stretching his arms.

'I'll take leave now,' Hiya said.

'See you next week,' I said. Our eyes met.

'Right, bye then,' she said shyly as she walked away.

'She smiles a lot,' Vihaan said.

'Yes indeed. She doesn't speak much either.'

'You like her dog very much, right?' Vihaan asked. I shook my head. 'There are chances that you like her too.' He looked at me.

'What do you mean by… like?' My concentration drifted from gazing Hiya to Vihaan.

'Like… like her… you know, affection…'

'What! No way,' I replied before he could finish speaking, and I walked towards my scooter.

'She seems like a nice girl.' Vihaan followed my steps and sat on his bike.

'The only person who needs a girlfriend right now is you.'

'The hunt is going smoothly.' He smiled widely and ignited the engine.

'Hope you get one soon.'

Hiya

The universe has a 13.7 billion-years history and is full of mysteries. Galaxy, stars, planets, comets, asteroids, nebulas, and the list continues. The universe is a great, big, fat family. Whenever I lay my head down to stare at the sky full of stars, it makes me realise that I don't just belong to a man-made territory. I also belong to this Earth, a very beautiful planet with mountains, rivers, oceans, deserts, glaciers, animals, and birds. Not just I, but we all belong to the address of Milky Way Galaxy, the universe.

Hindus worship different stars and planets. Technically, they are worshipping the great universe, and that's really beautiful. When it comes to believing in God, I have my beliefs. I believe in prayers. They are powerful and hold an enormous amount of positive vibes and energy.

I wish I could travel to different planets just like we travel to different places on earth. I wish we could go without a spacesuit to explore the vastness of the universe. I wish I could walk on the Saturn rings and see how big Jupiter is with my naked eye. I wish I could visit different galaxies. The only thing I can do is make a wish. But wishing or thinking about these things brings me sheer joy. I am a night owl who can stay awake late to witness the glory of the night. Days are all similar in their boring daily routines.

I had midterm exams at the beginning of the week. I belong to the team of students who read just a night before the exam, and midterm exams were the least thing I care about. When I came out after giving the exam on Saturday, the rain touched the earth again. Why didn't God create super-absorbent soil that would consume water instantly like a sponge?

Vihaan's text message to be present at the class flashed up while I was eating lunch with Doodle, sitting on the chair next to me, trying to figure out what I was eating. There must be thoughts running through his little mind about how I can eat and digest different colours and varieties of food.

Ma woke me up from sleep at 3:30 in the evening. She had prepared tea for all of us. I sipped mine, grabbed my backpack.

I waited in the parking lot, sitting on my scooter, keeping an eye on all the vehicles like a hawk. There was no sign of the people I was looking for. I waited for another five minutes, and I saw Arnav and Vihaan riding together on a bike, both wearing casual t-shirt and jeans.

'So early,' Vihaan said.

'More like right on time!' I replied. Unlike me, they had no backpack with them. I carried a 200-page notebook, a pen, my wallet, and a water bottle with me.

'What do you think of doing post-graduation in Structure, Hiya?' Vihaan asked breaking the awkward silence in the lift.

'No, I honestly am not good at all,' I replied.

'What?' Arnav and Vihaan's voices echoed.

'Then what are you doing in this field? I mean the foundation lies in the structure, right?' Arnav said.

'Exactly!' Vihaan added the same energy. The lift door got unlocked on the second floor. None of us moved till Arnav stopped the door getting closed again.

'Civil engineering has many doors that you can choose for post-graduation. Right?' My words shut their mouths. I felt happy about that. 'There are plenty of choices, you know.' I wanted to tell all the choices but stopped there.

'Correct,' Arnav said and let out a sigh. 'She got points you can't ignore,' he said to Vihaan.

Vihaan shook his hand with the person we met that day. He guided us to our seats. There were many students present in that place, operating different softwares. That person showed us the empty computer tables & asked us to choose the seats. Arnav and Vihaan rushed and chose the corner seat and Arnav won. Vihaan sat on the chair next to him but stood up suddenly as if he sat on spikes.

'Hiya, would you mind sitting next to this brilliant future architect?' Vihaan asked. 'If we'll sit together then we'll spend more time talking about useless things.'

'Anywhere is fine for me,' I said and sat on the chair that he was holding.

'Are you comfortable?' Arnav asked me. I shook my head and smiled.

'Hello everyone!' A person walked in and said. 'I am here to teach you the software. You all can call me Naveen,' he said.

'Nice to meet you, Naveen.' Vihaan approached first.

'Me too. So shall we begin?' He clapped and rubbed his hands. 'Introduce yourself in short. What's your name, young lady?'

'Hiya.'

'That's a sweet name,' he said. Everyone present in his class introduced themselves. Naveen started his lecture by talking about the software, from its history to its latest version. It took him nearly half an hour to complete his speech. Appearance and age wise he looked like a person in his late twenties. He had an expert level of knowledge about AutoCAD. Naveen shifted his chair next to Arnav's to teach him, which took more than half an hour.

There was too much creativity under one roof. From fashion design to character design to animation to technical design, and I always wanted to be part of such a creative environment. I felt glad and grateful that I got a chance to join this journey, not just for one reason but for many.

Arnav

I was waiting for my mother, who had taken my scooter for her grocery shopping. Soon I caught a glimpse of her riding on the scooter at a speed of twenty. She stopped her scooter near me. I hastily pulled down the bag full of vegetables and took the scooter in my hand.

Hiya came after me and was searching for a parking space. I moved my scooter a little so she could fit her vehicle. In a white t-shirt, blue jeans, a watch on her left wrist, flat sandals, and a ponytail, she looked simple and pretty.

'You are so punctual, aren't you?'

'It's just the fear of not getting any parking spaces, that's why.' she chuckled.

'Your remarkable thought deserves appreciation.' We took steps forward, talking. I saw her footsteps match mine.

'How is architecture treating you?' she asked when we walked inside the academy.

'Can we just talk about something more interesting on the weekend at least?' I sighed.

'Is it that bad?' She shot another question.

'Please don't ask. I'll start sobbing,' I said and saw Vihaan, who was present already. She giggled. My eyes shifted from Vihaan to Hiya. I laughed with her.

'Couldn't you tell me a little earlier?' I punched Vihaan.

'Risha told me at the last moment to drop her,' Vihaan said, rubbing his shoulder. 'That's why I couldn't come to pick you up.'

'Useless!' I said, taking my seat.

While I was practising some newly learned tools, Hiya's phone blinked. It was a text message from a person named Rahul. I couldn't read the message as my eyes promptly shifted on the wallpaper, her dog Doodle. I wished for her phone to blink again so that I could ask her about her dog. My words were ready to come out, but the phone wasn't responding to my wish.

She took the phone in her hand, finally. I was sure she was talking with the same person. Her typing speed impressed me. I kept observing her from the corner of my eyes. I wondered about the guy she was chatting with.

Who was he? Her friend? Best friend? Or… Boyfriend? Hiya doesn't seem like a girl with a boyfriend. She is too shy to have a boyfriend. What they would talk about? But shyness of a person depends on with whom they are talking. There are people with whom we feel most comfortable talking, and on the other hand, there are people whose faces we can't tolerate. Hiya has the right to like and dislike whoever she wants. What am I thinking, and where am I heading? I gripped my mouse and concentrated on my software.

'Arnii… Can you please come here? I pressed something, and it changed the settings,' Vihaan said at the same time when I was about to open my mouth to talk with Hiya.

'Am I the one who teaches here?' A little annoyed, I said.

'No, but you know this software. Come here, bro.' Typing random keys on the keyboard, Vihaan requested.

I solved his problem within seconds, like magic. Vihaan was impressed with my knowledge. Hiya seemed fascinated as well.

'Now get back to your seat. Don't roam here and there. This is not a garden,' Vihaan ridiculed.

'Leaving so early?' I asked, watching Hiya turn off the computer.

'I have to visit the pet store to buy food for my dog,' she replied.

And I found my perfect question. I knew Vihaan won't be interrupting as his intelligence about dogs and animals is in the negative. F minus, if I have to rate him.

'Can I join you? I asked hesitantly. Vihaan, whose face was fixed in front of the computer screen, turned towards me. He was staring at me with suspicious eyes. Our eyes met, and I gave him a tiny smile. Hiya happily agreed.

'Want to join?' I asked Vihaan. I knew he wouldn't say yes at any cost.

'I appreciate the invitation, but I'm not interested,' he said, without looking at me.

'Well then, see you later, brother.' I patted his shoulder.

'Hope the dog chases you,' he shouted. I heard his taunt from the reception. I raised my thumb.

* * *

'Are you just a dog person, or do you like other animals too?' I asked when we were standing side by side to cross the road.

'I love the whole animal kingdom,' she said excitedly.

The road was very busy, and it was hard to listen what she was saying in her slow voices. I bent down a little so that I could hear her clearly.

'I grew up watching Disney movies where all princesses are animal lovers and have one sweet pet. I was deeply influenced by it,' she said.

'So with a Doodle you feel the same way?' I asked.

She nodded. 'With my Doodle, I feel like one of those princesses that talk with their pets for expert advice.' She giggled.

We had to cross the road, which was busy with constantly moving vehicles. 'When I say run, you follow,' I held her hand and said. She agreed. 'Run.' We ran and reached on the other side.

'Animals are better than humans,' she said. I noticed her excitement level doubling whenever she got a chance to speak about animals.

'You're an introvert who can't say hi to any human freely but can sing a song with an animal without any language barrier, right?' I pushed the door inside and let her enter first.

She agreed. 'No language is needed. It's just the purest connection of two hearts that requires warmth and actions only,' she said before entering.

Though it was a noisy atmosphere outside, my ears caught all the words that she spread.

'Are you buying anything?' She asked me.

'Not really but I think I'll definitely end up buying something.' I said, observing the whole place.

'Just like me. My bills are higher in pet shops than clothing stores,' she said.

There was a baby Labrador, a baby Pug, and a Persian cat available in the store. The Labrador baby rushed to me. Hiya lifted the little one. The puppy was so playful. It just took a few seconds to create an eternal bond between Hiya and the puppy that humans would take years to create with other humans. She was completely involved with the puppy. The way she was talking with the puppy, I couldn't stop smiling.

'It's Coco and it'a girl,' the owner of the shop came and said.

'So tasty and yummy,' she said, embracing the puppy.

'Take her home with you,' the owner insisted.

'Oh, then I'll have to buy a new home first to live with all the dogs I adore and wish to live with.' she chuckled.

We laughed at her silly comments. She took food for her Doodle, and I bought a leash for my Cookie. We paid our bills separately.

Hiya

I like to revisit the past, especially the good memories. Arnav seemed like a nice person to talk with. I always like people with whom I can freely talk about my pet, other animals, birds, space, the stars, and the universe, and Arnav fits into that category. I never asked him about his dog. I promptly inspected his social media profiles. There weren't many photos of his dogs. His photography was close to being professional. The more I explored his other social media profiles, the more reasons popped up in my mind to talk with him about his likes and dislikes, beliefs and disbeliefs, perceptions and dreams. I wanted to know everything about him.

I was already present in the class when someone pulled the main door. I saw Arnav and Vihaan through the transparent glass placed as divisions. My mind stopped functioning when I saw Arnav. My curiosities were bouncing within me. In a matter of seconds, I imagined myself grasping Arnav's hand and taking him to an isolated room and interrogating him the questions that were waiting for an answer. My hand sensed a sudden coldness. I inhaled deeply to control my senses. The smell of his perfume felt so good to my nose.

'Hiya, how do you manage to come on time so perfectly?' Vihaan asked.

Vihaan's words diverted my mind. 'Guess my clock shows me the right time.'

'I like your sense of humour,' Vihaan laughed. 'Exams finished?'

'Yes. so relieved,' I said.

'I am good at structure and I give door-step services,' Vihaan smirked. 'So if you need any help, you can ping me anytime.' Vihaan added. Arnav gave a sharp and doubtful look.

Naveen appeared with a bunch of flyers in his hand. He distributed the flyers to everyone present in the class. 'We have an event coming up. I am thrilled and happy to tell you that you guys can participate, too.'

It was a dark blue glossy flyer with a bold and big title, 'The Stop Motion Battle' and a tagline, 'Let the Race Begin'. Below that was a splash of different colours, and on that was a camera with a reel. A few instructions were written below the image, and at the end of the flyer, important information like a contact number, website, and a few more things were written.

'You must be thinking how this is relatable to you, but friends, creativity knows no restrictions, no territories, and no age limit,' he said cheerily.

'Sounds interesting!' I heard someone say when I was busy reading the flyer.

'Indeed!' I announced without noticing whose energy I joined. That was Arnav.

'Yes! I look forward to such energy,' Naveen said, pumping up his fist. With two talented artists on board, who else is joining?'

Vihaan and all the other members present in the room showed their interests.

'Each team will have four or five members, depending upon the count of participants,' Naveen explained. 'Are you all electrified?' He clapped.

'Yes!' We all said it loudly.

'Amazing! Let's begin today's lecture.'

Arnav

From the split between two curtains, the sun-rays fell on my face. The warm sensation on my cheek sent a message to my mind, and I moved myself into the shadows. I felt a vibration from the phone in my pocket. My eyes struggled to open up. Before I could pick up the call, it stopped vibrating, and I slept again. The sun-rays hit me again, harder this time. I tried to gain my memories, which I felt like I had lost completely. The last thing I remembered was writing my assignment.

When my eyes were fully awake, I realised that I had fallen asleep while writing the assignment. The papers and pen were still in my lap. My phone vibrated again.

The lecture has started. It was a message from my classmate. I pulled myself up promptly. The assignment papers on my lap swung in midair. I brushed my teeth, washed my face, changed my t-shirt, and ran. The lecture had already begun, and I was fifteen minutes late.

'Where were you?' My friend asked.

'I was working late and couldn't wake up,' I said, aiming to catch the professor's words. 'What lecture is this?' I asked, confusingly.

'Building Construction, next is history.'

'Brilliant, I'll go and come back later,' I said. 'I haven't bathed for two days, and my assignment is also incomplete.' I escaped before my history professor could catch me.

I felt so fresh bathing after two days. I came back to college and went to the canteen. I was famished. My classmates were already there, waiting for me, discussing *Ganpati celebration*. I brought a plate of dry Manchurian for me and joined them. Be it *Holi*, *Navratri*, or *Ganpati*, we celebrate all the festivals with great joy.

* * *

My fellow passenger on the train woke me up, saying the next station was mine. In half an hour, I had the best sleep of my entire week. The train passed through the bridge over the *Purna* River. I saw the most splendid cloud formation, looking like golden cotton balls, from the window. The sun's rays were coming out, tearing the clouds. I captured that moment on my phone. I had called Vihaan to pick me up from the railway station.

'Can't you walk any faster?' He taunted me the moment we met.

I, who was carrying a big backpack hanging on my shoulder, a duffle bag full of clothes, and a sheet holder, gave him a very grumpy look. Without saying a word, I took the pillion seat. He stared at me for my silent act. Before reaching the art academy, I dropped all of my luggage at home.

Vihaan stopped to check the list of students. I, who didn't notice, took my steps back.

'He put Hiya in our team!' I was surprised.

'We are going to annoy her so much,' Vihaan giggled.

'Don't think of that. She'll start crying.'

I noticed that each team had four members, but my team only had three. I raised my query with Vihaan.

'Actually, he is not participating anymore,' Naveen, standing behind us, replied. 'He stepped out at the last minute, and there are no more people left to add.'

He assured to help us when in need. We got Naveen as a mentor and that was enough. Hiya had come already as usual.

'You're one of us now,' Vihaan said, shaking Hiya's chair. She got scared.

'Trust me, you've got the best teammates,' I winked, looking at Vihaan.

'The best entertainers as well,' Vihaan added.

'Any ideas for the story?'

'What story?' absent-minded Vihaan asked.

'Story for the contest,' Hiya replied. She must have wondered if Vihaan is dumb or what. I would have agreed with her that Vihaan can present his stupidity anytime, anywhere.

'Let's gather at your place, and we'll wrap up the story idea first. What do you say?' I suggested pointing a finger at Vihaan.

'Sure,' Vihaan concurred without any hesitation. We both looked at Hiya for her response. Reading her face, I knew she was about to say no.

'No excuses,' I declared. 'You're part of the team, and you'll have to come to Vihaan's villa.'

'Its bungalow not liva…I mean villa.' Vihaan corrected.

We both convinced her. As far as I got to know her in the last few weeks, I could tell by reading her face that she agreed because she had no other choice. Vihaan reminded her again to reach his place on time when she was leaving the academy. She nodded as if we commanded her to do it.

'Do you really think that she'll come?' Vihaan asked me.

'I think so and hope so,' I replied.

'Why my home and not yours?' Vihaan asked.

I sighed and looked at him. 'My parents are not home tomorrow,' I explained. 'Wait, your parents will be there, right?'

'Yeah, I mean, if not my parents, Risha will be there,' Vihaan answered. 'No one can tolerate her more than five minutes.'

'Please tell Aunty to make her tasty corn fritters. It's been so long.'

Hiya

They left me no choice. I was riding back home on my scooter, and my brain was busy imagining scenarios. I was barely concentrating on the road when a rider ahead of me applied the brakes so suddenly. I pressed my brakes quickly to save me and my scooter.

I could have said no so easily. It feels awkward to go. I've never been to any friend's house except Kavya's. She should have joined the classes with me. But why would she join when the software is as useless for her as the guitar I have but don't know how to play a single beat. I forced my father to get me a guitar after I got 85 percent in my 10th board exams. *If I'd suggested my home, it would have been less awkward. Why can't such brilliant ideas come to mind when in need?*

All my worries were wiped away when I saw my precious paws waiting for me eagerly, started jumping around me as I showed myself to him. But it knocked again when Vihaan sent me his home location. *Will it work if I come up with an excuse to avoid it? I can lie and say that I have an appointment with the vet. I hope they understand how hard this simple task is for me. I can come up with a story idea by sitting in my room as well. I can share my ideas through text. Why won't this shyness leave me alone? I am such a weird person to fit in the human category.*

Humans are social animals; they talk, act, and react. I am human too. Shyness is one of those inbuilt features in some people like an android phone; it's useless but you can't remove it.

Please come tomorrow. It'll be fun. Don't be shy. Arnav sent me the text.

It's just that I haven't been to anyone's house like this before. I replied back. I instantly regretted sending a brainless message.

Oh, come on! We are not anyone, okay!! We are friends.

My eyes stuck on that message for a while. *We are friends.* I couldn't let that sentence out of my mind. I was blushing and smirking alone in my room. That one short sentence boosted my confidence. I assured him that I would be there. I re-read the whole chat again and again till my heart was satisfied.

* * *

Discovering Vihaan's house wasn't that hard. *'Aashray'* was the name of his house as per his given address. I saw a white bungalow behind white wooden gate. A row of Ashoka trees were planted outside the bungalow. The hinges squeaked as I unlatched the gate at a snail's pace. I saw the white Mercedes in the parking lot, which reminded me of my luxurious ride. I made my way to the main door and rang the doorbell. A girl opened the door and I asked for Vihaan.

'Jiya right?' She said, opening the door fully.

'Hiya,' I corrected her with a smile. Often, people mispronounce my name.

The house was pretty big. On my right was the living room, with white paint and pale brown recliner leather sofas placed on glazed vitrified tiles. A marble-topped coffee table was put on the woollen floral carpet. One of the four walls was decorated with floral grey wallpaper. On my left was an open space, and in the centre was a six-seat dining table.

'I am Risha. Idiot Vihaan's genius sister,' she said, leading me towards the dining area. I saw a big glass door from the dining area with a garden view.

Vihaan, from behind me, came down the spiral staircase. 'Hey ya, Hiya,' he said, and stood next to me. 'Everyone knows who the genius in this house is,' he said giving a competitive look to Risha.

'Stop you two,' someone from the kitchen shouted. I guessed it before Vihaan introduced his mother to me. She welcomed me warmly.

The glass door clattered. I turned to see who walked in. 'That's my father.' I recognised him, too. His father was carrying some gardening tools in his hands which were covered with mud. He shared a gentle smile and made his way to his room. Vihaan led me to his room saying Arnav had come earlier.

Climbing the last step, I saw a common area connecting three doors. *Arnav is inside.* My heart said following Vihaan's footsteps. Vihaan's room was well equipped with a king-size bed, a cupboard, a study desk, and a two-seater couch with a small centre table. I saw Arnav sleeping on the couch, uncomfortably, with papers and a pen with him.

'What a rare visual. A sleeping architect!' Vihaan pulled out his phone and clicked a photo of Arnav. He woke up hearing the sound.

'I want to sleep for twelve nonstop hours.' Arnav complained with a tired look.

'You've got a story idea, or were you dreaming about it?' Vihaan asked.

'Hiya, what about you?' Arnav asked me instead of replying. He made a place for me next to him by gathering all his belongings. I was also answerless just like him.

'We need to finalise the story by today,' Vihaan said, struggling to pull out his laptop from his backpack. 'Bro, I got your favourite series's episodes.'

'Great! I'll complete it tonight,' Arnav exclaimed.

'Someone wanted a constant twelve hours of sleep!' Vihaan mocked, passing the pen drive to Arnav.

'Keep up the good work.'

Both boys were talking about the series instead of the story. Risha walked in with a big tray in her hand. She brought a plate full of corn fritters and other snacks.

'Would you mind bringing a glass of water for us?' Vihaan ordered, sounding more like he was teasing.

'Why not, sir! Anything else you want?' She retorted.

Arnav and I were enjoying the scene and were hiding our smiles, looking at each other frequently. In the midst of the argument, their mother entered the room with three glasses of orange juice. She warned Vihaan not to quarrel with Risha.

'Can… we concentrate on the story please? Arnav tried to break the argument.

When Vihaan's mother and sister left, we concentrated on the story and snacks. The fritters were delicious. For half an hour, none of us spelled a word except Vivaan, who kept murmuring every five minutes, complaining that writing a story was a hard thing to do for him.

'Ok. I have one story,' Arnav said, adjusting papers. 'With your suggestions, we can finalise.'

'That seems easy. You're a genius,' Vihaan said, excitedly.

In one small town, a six-year-old boy was living with his parents. One day, they all went to the park. The boy demanded a packet of chips. His father got him one. While eating, a few chunks fell to the ground. The boy didn't bother to take it. After some time, he saw the ants carrying chunks. The boy showed it to their parents.

'Do you know that these ants are very hardworking and they never stop running?' His father said. Later, he told the boy about the qualities of ants, like how they work as a team, their discipline, and their hard work. 'You can learn so many things from everything you see and feel,' the mother added. 'Always remember that patience, discipline, and hard work are the primary keys to making your life successful.' The boy listened carefully to their parents' words.

When he ran to play in the garden, he saw kids fighting over who would go first on the sliding ride. The boy recalled the ants following the queue. The boy asked the children to make a queue so that everyone could get a chance. His father saw how he managed the situation based on the given advice. He raised his thumbs, and the boy gave him a big smile in return. While returning home, his father gave him an ice cream treat for his brave effort.

Arnav stopped speaking. 'Any suggestions?' He added.

'It's good,' Vihaan said. 'We can show some more scenes that show discipline and hard-work.'

'What's your story?' Arnav asked Vihaan and he showed the blank paper.

Their faces turned to me. The four eyes that were staring at me, made me nervous. I knew they wanted to hear my story, but I was not confident.

Arnav

I took the paper from Hiya's hand. 'At least you've tried something, not like this idiot who shamelessly showed me blank paper.' I threw my pen at Vihaan. He argued in return. 'Shut up. You're useless,' I scolded him. 'If by chance we win, only you and I are going to share the winning prize, okay?' I said to Hiya.

'I'll help you prepare the model, happy?' Vihaan suggested.

I ignored him and read Hiya's story instead. 'This is far better than mine, Hiya. I think we should go with this one,' I said after reading her story. Hiya was confused, as if I was joking. I gave the paper to Vihaan and asked him to read it out loud.

Once upon a time, there lived a family of a mother, a father, and their little daughter. One day, the girl came from school and, as usual, started asking questions. Her mother was answering all her silly questions happily. She excitedly told her mother everything. Suddenly she stopped speaking, and her mother looked at her.

'Is helping people a good thing, mother?' she asked out of curiosity. 'Yes, indeed,' her mother answered. The girl said that her teacher taught them the importance of helping each other in life. The mother held her daughter's hands and said, 'Help

and hope can change the world.' The little girl was gazing into her mother's eyes curiously. 'When you help everyone, it changes their world, and when you have hope alive inside you, it changes your world.'

The mother placed her daughter on her lap. 'No matter how bad the situations become in life, never stop helping people and never let the hope inside you die. Then you'll be the happiest person in this life.' The next day, after coming from school, she helped her mother in the kitchen and her father too. She told them how she helped her friends at school.'

'I'm still thinking about how to end it,' Hiya replied.

'I don't think we need one,' I interrupted. 'We need a good concept, and we have it. We don't need narration, we need action. *Hope and help can change the world.* This line will work as the moral of the story.'

'Yeah, it's not a writing competition,' Vihaan said. 'Well done, Hiya. Never knew you were such a good storyteller.'

Our plates were empty, and it was almost time to go. I packed my bag. Hiya helped clean up the place. She took the plates, and I took the glasses. Aunty had really made delicious snacks.

The visuals were different as soon as we stepped in the academy. The place was busier than ever before. Most of them were students of the academy. I saw a big banner hanging on the wall that read 'The Stop Motion Battle.' I realised that all of these people were participants. The atmosphere was noisy, and the songs running in the background made it more annoying.

Naveen spotted us and asked us about our story. He invited us to join him in his cabin. The loud noises stopped bubbling once I closed the door. I showed Hiya's story first and mine later.

'Interesting, both of them. You're free to pick any,' Naveen stated.

'We'll go with Hiya's story,' Vihaan said.

'Great! I read really good stories today. It's going to be a very exciting competition.'

Naveen explained the next procedure. Looking at the atmosphere in the place, none of us seemed interested in learning about software tools. But Naveen came out to be a strict teacher in those terms.

We three went to our original place and discussed a few things. Vihaan proved to be the laziest team member once again. My first experience was in school, when our physics teacher gave us a project to do, which I did alone. We prepared a temporary draft of the scenes, dialogues, and narration we wanted to include.

'Next week, you can start preparing models. Give your list to the receptionist and she'll arrange all the materials,' Naveen said. I had to inform him about the festival celebration that I was going to attend in my college. He gave me permission to go without any questions.

* * *

'You can make the list of needy things ready till I come back,' I said to both, standing in the parking-lot.

'Don't teach us what to do. You go and enjoy your celebration. Am I right, Hiya?'

She agreed with Vihaan.

'I never expected this from you, Hiya. I thought you were my friend first, then Vihaan's.' I complained.

'There is no first and second. She is my friend equally, and she is on my side.' Vihaan argued.

'Hiya, you're on my side, right?' I walked near her aggressively.

'No one. I am on nobody's side,' baffled Hiya said, taking her steps back.

'No, you will have to choose, and you will not come next week, ok?' I had scared her enough, and that was clearly visible on her face.

I and Vihaan looked at each other, hardly controlling our laughs.

'See, that's the exact face I had imagined.' Vihaan let out his laugh.

Hiya couldn't understand what was happening to her. She was astonished.

I put my hands on her shoulders. 'We're just teasing you,' I said.

'You're so naive, Hiya,' Vihaan squeezed her cheeks.

An awkward smile covered her face. Before our prank could go wrong, we both apologised. I had doubts that she would start crying, but she didn't.

With loud music, a group of people passed on the main road carrying an idol of Lord *Ganesha*. It was beautifully crafted, and it drew many people's attention around us. The kids were dancing with joy. Seeing such a majestic idol, many people joined their hands and prayed. I saw Hiya doing the same thing.

'What's your favourite festival?' I asked her later.

'Diwali,' she replied.

'Mine too,' I said. 'I like all the festivals, whether it's kite flying, Holi…'

'Don't forget *Navratri*.' Vihaan jumped in our debate.

'Must be on the list of every Gujarati,' I said, agreeing. 'Do you know what the secret is to Vihaan's thin, skeleton-like body?' I asked Hiya.

'Shut your mouth…' Vihaan attempted to stop me. I easily removed his hands from my face.

'He can play *Garba* for four nonstop hours.' I struggled to complete my sentence as his hand kept stopping me. She laughed.

'That's because it comes once a year and for nine days only,' Vihaan clarified.

'Do you go somewhere to play Garba?' I asked Hiya.

When she denied, we looked at her as if she said something unworthy.

'You can't call yourself a Gujarati if you don't play Garba!' Vihaan declared.

'I play, but not on an extreme level,' she explained.

'You're going to come with us where we go to play, and I will not listen to any NO.' Vihaan showed excitement as if he would start teaching Hiya at the very moment. Vihaan promised to bring her a pass.

'We'll see. I've to go now.' She dashed away before we pressured her more.

'You scared her, man!' I said.

'Yeah, her face though,' Vihaan laughed.

'I thought she would start crying.'

'The same thoughts crossed my mind.'

'She will become tough after working with us,' I chuckled.

'Or she will avoid meeting us once we finish the classes.'

Hiya

Idiots, Maniacs. Both of them. The fumes of the prank didn't leave my mind, like the scene had been put on repeat telecast mode. I was attending the last lecture of the day. My eyes were staring at the blackboard, but I was physically present and mentally absent. When the bell rang, Rahul woke up my mental state.

'Were you daydreaming?' He asked.

'Yes, maybe,' I packed my backpack.

'What about our movie plan?' Rahul asked me and other friends. 'Let's go this weekend,'

'I have class to attend,' I said.

'Take leave for one day then!'

'But…' I stopped there and exhaled. 'I'll let you know. Bye.' I rushed to the bus.

I am not a prank-friendly person. I never was part of that community, which play pranks and laugh endlessly. My shy and sweet personality would never let me do something like that. A few more minutes with them, and my tears would've rolled down my cheeks.

Arnav expressed his regret that night as well. Our chat continued till late at night, and he described how he and Vihaan plotted the web against me. He asked me about my studies and my dog and also explained why I should go for a master's degree in structural engineering. His motivations didn't raise a single curiosity in me.

I hope you're not mad at me anymore. He mentioned it again. I liked the way he kept apologising, which wasn't necessary. It made me feel special. Rereading our old chat became my habit. That's the power of writing; unlike speaking, it stays with you and is at your service when you want it. Deep down, somewhere in the little corner of my heart, the thought of *not seeing him for the next few days* ached me a little. Listening to Arnav and Vihaan's conversations, even though many of them are beyond my understanding, had become a routine.

Later that night, I and Doodle spent some quality time on the terrace after so long. The sky was cloudy, though. I couldn't find planets and stars in the sky, but watching the moon play hide and seek with the black clouds was relishing. Doodle, head resting on my stomach, dozed off taking head massages. I wanted to write something in my diary, but the words were playing hide and seek with my mind, too. I was occupied with so many thoughts. Every day in my life brought me new experiences, and I made it to the most of them. With a pledge that I made for myself not to nurture *any hard feelings,* I wanted to dive deep into those moments and save the precious pearls till my heart stops pulsing.

Rahul had made a plan for a movie on Saturday. I had denied it already. The timings were not convenient for me, as I and Vihaan had decided to go early to take our seats before the place becomes overcrowded. Moreover, I never found that movie trailer catching.

* * *

Please let me know whatever happens in my absence. Arnav sent me a message. Unfortunately, the phone wasn't in my hand and was within Vihaan's range. He read the text first and compelled me to open. He took the phone from my hand. I didn't know what he was typing, but examining his vicious smile, his expression assured me that I was in trouble, my reputation was in trouble, and my inner peace was in trouble. My efforts to rescue my innocent phone from Vihaan's hand failed because of the height issue. *I should have consumed two glasses of Complan every day!*

'Give my phone back,' I said expressing my anger.

'Just a second, sweetie! I am almost done,' he said, seizing my hands. 'He's smart and will figure out who sent it.' He made me sit on the chair, calming down my anger. I checked my phone to see what jumble he had created for me.

It's none of your business, and why the hell should I report you? I am not your assistant. If you've so much yearn to know, then come here and see with your own eyes. Stop irritating me and get lost.

The message was sent already. Arnav was online and was typing something. In a fraction of a second, my thoughts reached new heights. I wished to apply Ctrl+Z to my life.

The next minute, my phone screen was gleaming with Arnav's call.

'Pick it up!' Vihaan exclaimed. I hit the green button.

Hey Hiya! I know that it wasn't you and never can be; I trust you on that. Arnav spoke softly. *Please do me a favour and pass this phone to Mr. Vihaan. I know he's around. I would like to exchange a few words with him.*

Vihaan took my phone before I could give it to him. 'It's man to man talk. Your ears might burst, so I am going outside,' Vihaan mumbled near my ear, gave a broad smile, and strolled away. 'Your phone is in safe hands.' he came back to inform me.

At first, I was mad, but weighing over the thought of these two best friends' harmony, it dissipated. I wish I had someone, just like these two, who would fight with me and fight for me. That person will need so much patience until I come out of my comfort zone to speak ultimately, and that might take years.

It's a fast moving world we're living in, and with the technologies upgrading at rocket speed, we, the humans, cannot afford to stay behind. The irony is that humans introduced technology to rule the world, and the verdict came out that the technology making humans its puppets. It's a nice-looking thread that can connect us and also pose a breakneck threat that can shatter us.

'See! I told you he would catch me within seconds,' Vihaan said, giving back my phone. 'You put so much pressure on yourself. Relax!' He sat next to me.

I was feeling guilty for shouting at him. 'Sorry, I didn't mean to.'

'Don't be. I don't even remember what you said.' He took the paper from my hand. 'The good thing is I got to hear your real voice.' He winked. I smirked.

There was a missed call from Kavya. It reminded me that I had to meet her at the Phoenix Cafe. We hadn't gossiped together in a long time.

Arnav

I was struggling to catch my breath and calm my racing heart. I bent down and supported my hands on the knees. My classmate came out of the crowd searching for me. I couldn't hear a single word spoken by him because of the music playing in the background. He pulled me, and I couldn't resist. I began dancing madly to the beats with more force. Students kept spreading powder colours in the air.

We danced for nonstop one hour, and at last the small and self-made idol of Lord *Ganesha* we submerged into a pit on the college campus. I was coated with different colours from head to toe and looked like a rainbow. I immediately ran to my apartment to occupy the bathroom. It took half an hour to bring back my original skin colour. I was exhausted, and my whole body was demanding for a massage. I flattened myself on the bed and closed my eyes.

The room was dark. I couldn't see anything. I rolled my hands on the bed in search of my phone. My eyes squeezed dealing with sudden screen light. It was eight in the evening. I heard noises coming from the kitchen. It took effort to get myself out of bed. I went to the kitchen and found my cook, preparing fried rice for dinner. I asked him to make me a bowl of soup as well. My head was aching. I regretted dancing like a madman. *Maybe I'll feel better if I massage my head with hair oil.* I thought.

The spicy soup did its job, and my head was behaving normally. The spices added to the soup were so strong that they recharged my whole body. After much celebration, a pile of pending work and assignments had a deadline to meet. I was up until three in the morning to finish all my work. *I need to write down my cook's recipe for the soup.*

* * *

I won't be coming next Saturday.

I was eating lunch in the canteen when Hiya dropped a message on the chat group of software class. There was a photography workshop at my college on the same day, and I didn't want to miss that. After Hiya, I dropped message of my absence too. Vihaan fought with me in a private chat, and later he also decided not to go.

I came to know that Hiya was coming to Surat so I asked about her plans. Her purpose for visiting was some group project. I had plans to go home in the same evening after attending the workshop. I wanted to ask Hiya if she would like to join me on my journey home, as our stations were the same. *Should I ask her? Should I not? Yes or no?* I couldn't decide. *She is my friend. I can ask.* I asked her finally. The train she was going to take in the evening was the same train I travelled in every time. She agreed to go together with a clear and strict warning that if I came late, she'd leave me. I agreed to her terms.

On Saturday, for once, I thought to cancel my trip home and not to attend the workshop as well. I was tired and wasn't feeling well. My disturbed sleeping schedule and my back pain were getting worse day by day. I forcefully pulled myself together, ate the breakfast of *kanda-poha*, got ready, and went to the workshop. In the morning, Hiya again sent me a reminder to reach on time. I thought to tell her to come to my apartment in the evening but that seemed odd, so I sent her a meeting point convenient for both of us.

After attending the workshop, I ran to my apartment to pack the bags. It was 5:15 and Hiya had already called me twice. I stabbed all my clothes that needed laundry on an immediate basis, without folding them. When I was running on the road, my phone rang again. I knew it was her. I picked up the call.

Where are you? She asked me. I noticed the sense of tension in her voice.

In front of you. I replied, waving my hand from the other side of the road. In a baby pink t-shirt and blue jeans with a backpack hanging on one shoulder, she waved back. I crossed the road with all my luggage. A rickshaw stopped near us, and we both said at the same time, *railway station.* I let her go inside first as my luggage was bigger. She helped me fit all the bags inside properly.

'Are you leaving Surat permanently?' She asked while struggling to pull the bag inside.

'Not so soon,' I said, fitting myself in the rickshaw. Our heads collided while I was making an effort to adjust me and my luggage.

'Ouch,' she screeched, rubbing her head.

'Sorry,' I said, still fixing myself inside when my sheet box hit her head again. She didn't scream this time.

'Oh god, I am extremely sorry, Hiya.' My hands immediately ran to massage her head.

'It's okay,' She said, but wasn't looking though.

'Move faster,' I said to the rickshaw driver.

'I hope the train is on time,' she said.

'Well, this local is never on time, so you can just hope,' I said.

The struggle of pulling out the luggage remained the same when we got off the rickshaw. I paid the amount to the driver before Hiya could drag out her wallet. I lifted my bags and walked briskly towards the station when she stopped me.

'I have to buy a ticket,' she mentioned.

'Why? You don't have a pass?'

'I am not a daily traveller,' she retorted.

I placed my bags near her. 'You wait here, I'll go and get your ticket.'

The queue was long, and my rank was 8th. I saw her protecting my bags vigilantly so no one would walk over. While waiting for my turn, I overheard someone talking about the train getting cancelled. I looked on the digital screen showing train status, and my fear came true. The train was cancelled.

I checked the status of the next train, and it was a half hour late relative to actual time. I gave the news to Hiya.

'What do we do now?' She asked worriedly.

'I think we should…'

'Catch a bus. I was thinking the same,' she said.

'…take the next train. That's what I was about to say.'

'No. It'll be too late,' She replied worriedly.

'But I don't like to travel by bus.'

'We have no option, Arnav. I am taking the bus,' she argued.

'With this much luggage, I can't travel in government buses.'

'I'm taking the bus,' she stated sternly.

'I've got a first-class train pass,' I tried my best to stop her.

She gave me a grumpy look for my meaningless words. I exhaled deeply, lifted my bags again, and followed her. She took one duffle bag from my hand.

'What do you have in this? Stones?' She asked, measuring the weight.

'Bunch of unwashed clothes,' I answered.

The bus stand was within walking distance. It was noisier than a railway station. One bus was already there, ready for departure. There were no empty seats as we were the last passengers to ascend. A few unlucky people, like us, had no other option instead of standing.

Just after moving a few metres, the driver abruptly applied the brakes, throwing our body balance off. I promptly grasped the handrail. Hiya, who had my bag in her hand, lost her balance and collided with me. She clutched me tightly. We nearly embraced each other. My hand rushed to stop the person who was about to land on Hiya. I inhaled the fresh fragrance coming from her hair. Slowly she let go of me.

'That's why I don't like buses,' I said when she took her steps back. She took a hold on my bag again.

'I don't have any diamonds hidden in it. You can leave it for a while,' I said, taking the bag from her hand and placing it near my foot. She didn't react. She looked tired, but not more so than me. I rested my head over my hand holding the handrail.

'You look exhausted,' she said, noticing my eyes.

'I've slept barely for four hours since the last three days.'

'That's tough.' Her eyebrows were raised.

Her hair kept fluttering in the windy air. The sun was gradually saying goodbye to us. I looked for a vacant seat every time the bus stopped but didn't get success.

Hiya asked me about my workshop and gave me compliments on my photography skills. I asked her about her day.

'Well, my professor has distributed a few topics to make a presentation on, and it's a group project. My team members live in Surat.'

'So they made you come to their place.' I completed the sentence. She nodded. 'Do you like to travel alone?' I asked.

'Not really but If I have my doodle with me then I don't need anyone.'

'You love your doodle a lot, don't you?'

'Doodle is the best!' Her eyes were glistening while speaking.

We discussed all other dog breeds. She wanted a Siberian husky first but she dropped the idea because weather requirements didn't match. She showed me some videos of her Doodle. I showed her mine. We laughed a lot talking about the funny habits of our dogs. The conductor came and asked for the destination. I took two tickets and paid. Again, she refused to let me pay for her. I was persistent.

'You can give me a treat later,' I said, putting my wallet back in my pocket.

'What do you want?' She asked curiously.

'Maybe a plate of cheese and butter *locho* or a milkshake at Phoenix Cafe?'

'Sure!' She flashed a tiny smile.

She expressed her desire to meet my Cookie. I assured her to make a plan soon. A passenger sitting near us stood up. I placed my sheet box on the vacant seat and asked Hiya to sit. The other passenger advised both of us to sit down as he was leaving too.

'If you're free tomorrow, we can take our dogs to any park,' she said,

'Actually, I and Vihaan have a movie planned for tomorrow morning,' I replied. 'Tickets are cheaper, you know!'

A thought of asking her to join us popped into my head, but I was confused as to whether to ask or not. I asked her at last. After debating with herself for a while, she agreed. The sky was completely dark when we entered our city.

I didn't realise the distance of an hour with Hiya. I never heard her talk this much. Maybe my perception was wrong about her. She talks only when she has someone who will listen. She is full of life, but not in front of everyone; perhaps the chosen one. She doesn't speak nonsense. She has an affection for stars, which she mentioned while we watched the sunset from the window of the bus. She advised me as well to sometimes lay under the roof of stars as an alternative to a concrete ceiling. The bus stopped at the bus stand.

'You should thank me for advising you to take the bus; otherwise, you would be still waiting for the train,' she said coming out of the bus.

'I know,' I said, imagining myself waiting for the delayed train. 'My regards to your Doodle!'

'Mine to your Cookie.' We exchanged smiles and took steps in our respective directions.

Vihaan

All of a sudden, my plan got changed without my approval. I had purposely fixed my plan with Arnav. It made me confused and a bit angry. No offence, Hiya wasn't the problem but it was supposed to be just the two of us.

Hiya isn't joining us today. I read Arnav's text in the morning, and now that she was out, my plan was in. I had something important to discuss with Arnav. I explained to him when we met at the theatre.

'Two days back…'

'You scratched your father's Mercedes?' Arnav asked, assuming.

'No. I've not driven it in a long time,' I said annoyingly.

'Found Girlfriend?' He asked with sparkling eyes.

'She doesn't exist in my dreams. How am I supposed to have her in reality?' I blew air from my nose furiously. 'Any other guesses?' I asked. He denied it confusingly.

'Two days ago, I heard someone talking in the garden late at night. I heard from the balcony of my room.'

'Ghost?' Arnav mocked me, but I continued.

'I went to see. I had doubts about her, and I was right.'

Arnav was on the edge of knowing.

'That was Risha talking with her boyfriend over a call,' I said, displaying my devilish smile.

'How are you so sure?'

'Nobody on this earth is as smart as your sibling when it comes to researching and detectivity.'

'Does she know that you know?'

'Not yet. But I'll surely take some leverage from it,' I said, rubbing my hands.

'She is your sister, I hope you know.'

'I know, but his boyfriend will have to pass my test to enter my family.'

'That's overacting now.'

'Did you know that she took all my savings as a present on *Rakshabandhan*?'

'I feel happy being a single child sometimes watching you two.'

After coming out of the theatre, we had lunch in a restaurant and went to attend the class afterward.

'What made you cancel your plan at the last minute,' Arnav asked Hiya.

'Guests. My mother wanted my help.'

'Do you have a strict mother and father?' Arnav asked.

'My mother is stricter than my father,' she said.

'Have you ever spent a night at a friend's house?' I asked out of curiosity. She denied. It would've given me a shock if she'd said yes.

'What about *Navratri* passes?' Arnav asked, concentrating on his work.

'Yes. My father bought it yesterday. Thanks to my active mind, I took it before my sister could see it. So Hiya, you're coming with us.'

'No…'

'Girl, I didn't ask your permission. I declared that you're coming.'

'My parents will never allow me to roam till late at night.'

'You will be provided pick-up and drop-off facilities,' I said. 'Tell Kavya to join you. I'll arrange a pass for her.'

After so many buts, ifs, and excuses, she was convinced. We got Kavya's confirmation as well. So, I left her no choice. Strangely, Arnav was staring at Hiya while I was striving to get her ready. He wasn't helping at all. Naveen asked us to attend the classes one by one. He started with Hiya.

'You know, it's bad manners to gawk at someone,' I whispered in Arnav's ear.

'Gawk who?' He said changing his sight hastily.

'Don't act innocent. You were staring at Hiya, and you were looking stupid.'

'NO... I wasn't.'

I gave him a look that made him forget what to say. He was confounded.

'No Vihaan. It's nothing like that,' he said a little hotly.

'Then why were you staring at her?' I murmured.

'It's not what you think,' he said, knowing that nothing was going to satisfy me, but he went on. 'I was just observing the way you were making her uncomfortable enough to say no to you. I was trying to read her mind.'

'Oh really!' I raised my eyebrows.

'You know the mind of a silent person is a mysterious place. You can't predict.'

'So, you want to say my mind is pretty easy to decode because I talk too much,' I roared.

'Will you please stop it now?' He changed his seat furiously. I grinned over his act.

Arnav

'This is the home, right?' I confirmed with Vihaan. As per his declaration, we went to pick up Hiya on the first day of *Navratri*.

'Why is the streetlight not working?' Vihaan babbled and turned off the car engine.

'It's not that dark, though,' I answered, walking out of the car.

'Better we wait outside, what say?' Vihaan said, standing next to me.

Someone approached the main door. 'Yes, how may I help you?' he asked.

I assumed him as Hiya's father considering their facial resemblance. 'We are here to pick up Hiya, uncle… sir,' I replied softly, standing outside the gate.

'Are you out of your mind? He is not your teacher. Uncle is fine,' Vihaan muttered.

'Oh! Hiya's new friends. Come inside.' He welcomed us. 'How long will it take you? We will miss *aarti* on the very first day!' Uncle yelled. We got mistaken by his shout, and our feet stopped working. Later, we realised that he was talking to his wife.

'Papa!' I heard a voice, mixed with the noise of clinking jewellery. The voice came from above. Holding the gate, I looked up. Hiya was standing on the balcony. Since it was dark, I couldn't see her face clearly. I nearly dropped myself on the stairs looking up.

'Watch out!' Vihaan took a tight grip on my hand and saved me from falling.

'I missed the step,' I said.

'I know why. Normally, people look down while taking the stairs and avoid looking up.'

Hiya's mother came out. Uncle introduced her to us.

'Papa, give the spare key to my friends. I'll lock the door before leaving,' Hiya shouted from the balcony.

Uncle agreed. 'I am glad she has friends who convinced her to step out of home and enjoy the world,' he said.

For a few seconds, neither I nor Vihaan realised what to say. I thought her father would tell us to bring her daughter home on time.

'She rarely leaves the house for parties and fun. She just loves being at home all the time,' he added. I couldn't conclude whether her father was praising or complaining. Vihaan and I both looked at each other cluelessly.

'Don't be so late, okay?' Her mother warned and gave me the keys. The way she looked at us reminded me of Hiya telling us about her mother being stricter than her father.

'We'll drop her off on time, aunty. Happy *Navratri*!' I said.

'Happy *Navratri*,' she wished back and both left.

'I'll wait outside. You go and have fun with her dog,' Vihaan said, changing his mind at the last moment. I got excited over the thought of seeing her Doodle, which I had forgotten.

I entered the living room, which had milky white walls, an L-shaped sofa, a wall-mounted LED TV, an audio system, and some decoration. I walked ahead and saw the kitchen and one bedroom. I saw the stairs in front of me and went up. Out of the two rooms I saw, one was alive with light rays, fell on my shoes through the half-closed door.

Doodle barked at me as he saw me. She turned around suddenly. Her jewellery made the same clanking noise. For a moment, I stopped breathing, looking at Hiya. In a colourful, long Anarkali dress, she was looking attractive, and I was completely stunned. I forgot that her dog was barking at me. She came closer to stop Doodle's roar. The smell of her perfume travelled with her. She scolded Doodle for the bad behaviour. Her Anarkali dress swirled in all directions, where she was moving and I was standing still. She asked me about Vihaan.

'He is waiting in his car. He is afraid of you,' I said all in one breath.

'Me?' She asked confusingly.

'I mean… your Doodle.' On hearing his name, Doodle's ears woke up. 'He is very active,' I said, looking at her, trying not to stare.

'Why not! I call his name a thousand times a day,' she said happily. 'I am ready.' She adjusted her hair bun. I watched the reflection in the mirror. 'Did my father give you the keys?' Her eyes, with freshly painted eyeliner, looked at me from the mirror and asked.

I promptly changed my gaze before she could notice. She drew nearer to me. It unbalanced my heartbeats. She collected her watch from the bedside table behind me.

'Yes. I came to give it to you.'

'You could have given me in the car also.' She chuckled, looking for something.

'Yeah right,' I said, realising there was no need to come up.

She was hunting for her phone. I dialled her number. It buzzed beneath the pillow near me. I found it and gave it to her. The soft tip of her fingers touched mine.

'Come, Doodle, you'll be staying in the living room till I come back.' She took the soft, tiny bed in her hand.

'I thought you'd wear *lehnga-choli*,' Vihaan said to Hiya when we sat in the car. 'No doubt you look nice,' he praised, using words that I couldn't speak.

'Thanks. I'll wear it some other day.'

'So you'll be coming next time. I like that,' Vihaan said, roaring up the car engine.

'Can we go now?' Seeing the two talking like nothing else mattered irked me.

The *aarti* on the loudspeaker was roaring loudly. We could hear it from the parking lot. We picked up Kavya from her home, too. It was a big party plot converted into a *Garba* playing platform. We saw an idol of *Maa Amba* where a few people were performing the *aarti*. The ground was decorated with colourful lanterns, which were finely aligned in strings above our heads. A special stage was made for the team that sings *Garba*. A seat arrangement for the people who like to enjoy watching people play *Garba* was also made. A few food stalls in a corner were serving food varieties.

'Is this your first time here?' I asked Hiya, who was observing the decoration.

'Yes. I've heard a lot about this place.'

'Anyone else coming from our circle?' Vihaan asked.

'Nikhil is coming. We talked yesterday,' I reported.

On the stage, the singers were busy setting up different instruments.

'When will they start? It's already 9:30 in the clock.' Kavya let out her frustration.

I saw Nikhil and Mayank from where we were sitting. I waved at them. The big ground was filling up with people so fast. None of them could notice my hand. I called Nikhil and directed him to us.

The drums roared like a siren to alert everyone. One by one, different instruments synchronised into a powerful rhythm that automatically raised us from the chair to perform. People began entering, from all directions, in the big ring made to play *Garba*. In a matter of seconds, the first circle was filled with a chain of people. Another circle formed inside. One by one, five layers formed in ten minutes.

A group of people that perform *dodhiya* needs a space of five to ten feet, depending upon their energy level. The way these people twist their legs, take sudden turns, and fling their hands can tangle anyone's mind.

When the first round ended, I was soaked in sweat, and my red kurta had turned maroon. I drank a lot of water. Hiya, who was with me all the time, looked as fresh as I had seen her at home. We all ran out of energy and were hungry. There were counters of dosa, chaats, Chinese, milk shakes, and ice cream. We gave chances to all the food available there.

The second round started after fifteen minutes, and we gathered our energy back. That round ran for more than an hour. The police came to stop according to the guidelines as the clock was showing 12:30am and the first day ended well.

Hiya

I asked my mother to take some photos of my Doodle with me. The eighth day of *Navratri*, believed to be the most auspicious day among the nine days, was the reason I chose to wear traditional *Navratri* clothes. Doodle tried to eat my oxidised jewellery. It took lots of effort to stop him from doing idiotic things. I heard the familiar horn of a car while controlling Doodle.

I was astounded when I saw only Vihaan in the car. Vihaan, as if observing my mind, answered that he came to pick me up first as Arnav came late from college.

'You're looking cute in your outfits,' Vihaan complimented.

'You're looking good too,' I said, observing his blue kurta.

'If Arnav is not ready, do me a favour. Take the lift, press button five and snatch out that architect even if he is in his pyjamas,' he said, searching for parking.

'Why would I go? Bring your friend on your own,' I said.

A sudden anxiety covered me. Vihaan should have informed me at least two days before so that I would have gathered the courage to press the bell of Arnav's home. I advised Vihaan to call him. He followed, but Arnav didn't pick up.

'You'll get to play with his sweet little dog,' he urged. I couldn't resist him more. I came out and adjusted my clothes and ornaments. I was getting nervous with every step. I pressed five, and the lift moved upward. I stood in the centre of the corridor with four strange doors. I didn't know which one to knock. *Was there a list of name plates on the ground floor?* I heard a barking noise from one of the doors, and I got my answer. I spotted Arnav's shoes that travel with him, protecting his feet. I pressed the doorbell switch gently.

'I am so sorr...' I heard Arnav as he opened the door. 'Hiyaaa...' The shout scared me. He turned around suddenly. I couldn't understand what happened, and then my mind quickly went into the past and showed a few last seconds. The buttons of his black kurta were not tied and that's why he turned to fix it.

'I was expecting Vihaan but it's...' he stopped speaking as if something had forced him to. His eyes travelled from my head to toe. 'It's... you.'

'You look... amazing.' He stared at me. I didn't know how to react to his compliment and just smiled. It was awkward. I adjusted my ornaments again. He welcomed me into his home.

'Vihaan couldn't find a parking space,' I said taking a quick tour of his home.

From the living room to the dining area, it was wide open. By the size, I guessed it was a 3-BHK. The interior of his home looked so appealing and modern. The warm LED rope light illuminating from above the false ceiling was so soothing and calming. It was a bit dark, though.

'Come.' The moment he seized my hand and led me away, everything around me turned dark. 'What's wrong with the power?' He stopped briskly, and my head bumped into his back.

'Don't leave my hand,' I said, holding his hand tightly.

'I won't,' he said. 'We have power backup. It'll be back in three, two, and one.' The lights brighten the room. His cookie was barking continuously from the room in which she was locked.

'The day has finally come to introduce my Cookie to you.' He took a tight grip on my hand and led me. 'She is becoming stronger day by day.' His excitement was at its peak.

He asked me to wait outside till he cools down Cookie's temper. He slithered in and partly closed the door. 'Come inside,' he said after a minute.

I adore all dogs, but meeting someone else's dog is rare. I slowly opened the door and got lots of barks as a welcome. German shepherds are not easy to handle. I took a step back in horror.

'Easy girl! Easy,' he said, rubbing his Cookie. 'Come closer,' he said to me.

'I think I am good here,' I replied, still petrified.

'Come slowly and try to grab her attention.'

'I don't have any experience handling German shepherds.'

'She means no harm to you. Believe me! Just say her name.'

I called 'Cookie' gently and walked very slowly. She stared at me like, *'Hey you! How do you know my name? I haven't seen such face structure in my life.'*

'Put your hand slowly on her head and try to comfort her.' Arnav guided me.

I extended my hand, and the wagging tail told me, *'I like you, human!'*

She started jumping. I rubbed her head for a while. She enjoyed it.

'Apart from me and my parents, you're the first one whom she has accepted so quickly.'

'She is so cute, just like my Doodle.' I massaged her more efficiently. She put her paws on my shoulder and tried to absorb my smell.

'We should go before Vihaan's thoughts provoke him to leave us.'

I stood up. 'Your parents aren't home?' I asked.

'They have been to my uncle's house.' He took Cookie to another room. I waited for him in the living room.

* * *

'Sorry to keep you waiting man!' He told Vihaan.

'Have you guys decided together to wear black?' Vihaan asked us.

'No, that was by chance.' Arnav looked at his clothes and then mine. 'Same pinch!'

'Well then, by chance, today is the best dressed couple day and considering what you're wearing… all the best,' Vihaan said.

'Let's see then… who wins!' Arnav tied the seatbelt.

All school members were present when we arrived. They all assumed that I and Arnav wore the same colour on purpose.

'They're taking part in today's competition,' Vihaan mocked.

'No, the colours matched accidentally,' Arnav justified.

'So will be your stars someday!' Vihaan whispered the words in Arnav's ears, and I heard them, standing behind.

The feeling that I felt, the moment I heard those words, was strange. Something that I couldn't let out of my mind, and it kept repeating. I looked up at the night sky and saw a few stars twinkling.

The ground was packed with people. We somehow managed to enter the circle. I saw people wearing colourful traditional dresses. Many people were waiting in the queue to come inside and perform *Garba* on the most auspicious night.

The beats became faster, and so did our speed. I gave up early as to match their speed was impossible for me. Arnav was, as usual, soaked in sweat. He poured a bottle full of water over his head and face, then grabbed another to drink.

'I was so thirsty,' he said, throwing both bottles in the nearby trash can. He adjusted his wet hair. A few water drops landed on me and my clothes.

'Take a seat and enjoy the rest,' I advised.

'No way. The festival comes once a year. I must play.'

'Correct.' Vihaan appeared with plates full of dosas. Arnav took one plate from his hand. Vihaan asked me to hold another one so that he could go again and buy cold drinks. I ate one out of three pieces from Vihaan's plate. Later, I and Kavya brought plates of manchurian. The canteen was full of people and the ground was half empty. Vihaan grabbed the opportunity to click pictures.

'You all!' He shouted. 'Come closer, in one frame.' He unlocked his camera.

'Sure!' Arnav and Nikhil exclaimed like they were waiting. Everyone rushed to join Nikhil and Arnav. I was standing next to Vihaan.

'Hiya! Don't you want to be part of the big picture?' Nikhil asked. Vihaan pushed me towards the group.

'Come.' Arnav extended his hand as an invitation. I stood next to him.

'Please take photos of me and Arnav,' Vihaan said, giving me his phone. They made me click on twenty photographs.

'Now you two!' He said, taking his phone from my hand. I stood next to Arnav. He put his hand on my shoulder and dragged me closer. 'You guys really deserve a win today for best dressed couple,' Vihaan said, clicking the picture.

'What if we win today?' Arnav asked when Vihaan went to click other friend's pictures.

'There are so many beautiful real couples in here.' I said, looking around.

'So, do you think we're not looking beautiful together?' He asked with a raised eyebrow.

I couldn't figure whether he was asking this stupid question genuinely or was teasing me. 'We didn't dress as a couple.' I replied.

'But we are eligible for the category.' Arnav folded his hands as if he was enjoying my awkwardness. I smiled uncomfortably as I had nothing to say. 'You're out of answers. I know this because you start smiling when you've nothing to say.' Arnav read my mind there.

'We've no chance of winning today.'

'If we win today, you'll have to do what I tell you to do… compulsory.'

'And what if we don't?'

'I'll do whatever you say to do.' He chuckled.

'Are you gossiping about me?' Vihaan interrupted. The drums rang for the second round.

'You have no qualities that are worth gossiping,' Arnav replied and ran to join Nikhil in *Garba*.

In the end, they started announcing results. We came to know that registration was required to take part in any competition. I looked at Arnav with a victorious look. They announced three couples on the stage one by one.

'We found many non-registered people today wearing beautiful dresses, playing together, and we've chosen three out of them,' The judge said. To my surprise, the second name they called 'the black beauty couple', and the fingers moved towards me and Arnav. They called us on stage. All my group members cheered and clapped.

I wasn't prepared for this. If I had had a chance, I would have run away, but Arnav held my hand and led me to the stage. They gave us both a finely wrapped gift. I had never climbed the stairs of such a large stage in my life. The feeling was overwhelming. Though my mind continuously gave me the message that *you and Arnav are not a real couple, don't let this moment rule your head and heart.* But it was impossible for me to control my feelings, which knew no boundaries, knew no limitations, and knew no right and wrong.

I wasn't in my senses when the crowd was clapping for me and the man who I wanted to be with. I looked at him. He looked at me and held my hand. The touch created a spark in me. It all felt so real! I wished to have him at every step of my life. I wished for the stars to change our fate. I wished for the stars to come together to write our story.

Arnav

'So best couple, huh!' Vihaan started again after dropping Hiya off at home.

'Best-dressed couple, pronounce it properly.'

'It's all the same,' Vihaan said. 'So, what are you thinking now about her?' He asked.

'Thinking what?' I stopped singing the song I was mumbling.

'Hiya, who else?' Vihaan said. 'Honestly, you look good together. The way she was looking at you, I think she likes you.'

'Wait, slow down.' I told him to stop speaking, and he stopped the car. 'I mean to stop what you're thinking.' I turned to him. 'I don't think there is any chance, and there are no qualities in me that is like worthy.'

'Yes, there are,' he said, driving again.

'No, Vihaan. I don't want to. I am not a trustworthy person when it comes to commitment. I'm only committed to my goals and my future. I hope you're listening.'

There was a moment of silence in the car. I didn't even realise I'd reached home.

'Okay, I listened. But may I ask you a question?' Vihaan said. 'Honest answer only.' Vihaan warned. I allowed him. 'Do you like her?'

I was out of answers. Hiya's sweet, innocent smile telecast itself in front of me. Our memorable bus ride, the time I spent sitting next to her in the class, the flabbergasting moment when I saw her at the door of my home, looking like a doll that anyone would fall in love with. The way she was pampering my dog would be the very first quality I would search for in a life partner. I shut my eyes tightly and made a strong fist.

'No.' I nearly shouted. 'I mean…' I exhaled deeply. 'I don't think so.'

A serious silence dropped in. Vihaan looked confused at my answer, which I didn't justify.

'Ok brother. I understand you.' He assured me, sadly.

'Look, if I have said something to you that I shouldn't have…'

'Are crazy Arni? Nothing said by you will ever bother me, NOTHING!' He punched my shoulder. We shared a laugh.

'I can't imagine this seriousness between us. It's awkward.' I rubbed my shoulder.

'Yeah. It is,' Vihaan said. 'But… take it as advice or whatever you want…'

'Speak it, I won't mind.'

'Stay away… I mean keep a healthy distance from her… for her,' Vihaan said.

I nodded and sighed. 'Understood.'

'Now, it'd be a great help if you'll take yourself out of this fancy car so I can go home and get some sleep.'

'All right then, sleep tight.'

* * *

Do I really need to maintain a safe distance? I don't think I've feelings for her, then why keep my distance? She is my good friend. Does she really feel something for me? Why would she do that? I am sure she has more important things to think about. 'Stop thinking!' I mumbled and concentrated on my pen and paper.

What are you so afraid of,

When you're aware of your abilities.

What are you so scared of,

When you know your weaknesses.

I stopped my writing there. I was out of ideas. The biggest source of inspiration comes from the heart. My inner voice is my biggest source of motivation. But the inner me demanded sleep instead of waking up the poet's mind.

* * *

Vihaan finally had a conversation with her sister about her boyfriend. She was in shock when she found that Vihaan heard her talking with her boyfriend. Risha wanted Vihaan to meet her boyfriend. For that, Vihaan had taken leave.

That means only me and Hiya will be there. I thought. I wasn't paying attention during the lecture. We may not have won the 'best dressed couple' title, but we got a complimentary prize. *What can I tell her to do? A cup of coffee in the Phoenix Cafe? Or maybe I can offer some help in studies? Ask her to complete one of my pending drawings. A ride in a train from Surat to Navsari?*

Colourful clays, crayons, papers, cardboard sheets, pencils, and many other things were scattered everywhere. All the team members were running here and there for different materials. It wasn't a new thing for me. The atmosphere was similar to my college. Half of our model was ready. Hiya was neatly creating characters using clay. She was fully involved in her work.

'We don't require that much detail for the character's face,' I mumbled in her ear. The sudden voice scared her. The clay from her hand fell down. I picked it up and gave it back. I saw Vihaan, coming late.

'Were you supposed to come today?' I asked.

'It's tomorrow I am not coming,' he said and sat. 'Hiya. Do you need any help? Arnav is useless, I know that.'

'Half of the set is created by me!' I roared.

'Then why is it not finished?' He retorted. We continued arguing.

'Shut up, both of you,' Hiya screamed. We were stunned by her enraged face.

'Why are you mad?' I asked.

'I am unable to create this,' she complained and turned around.

'Give it to me. I'll do it,' I said, extending my hand. She placed all the material in my hand. I had never seen her lose her temper.

'I think Naveen is on leave today,' Vihaan said. 'I can leave early.'

'Do me a favour and just leave.' I taunted.

'I'll… when I WANT TO.' Vihaan retorted.

We both gave a competitive look to each other and then saw Hiya frowning at us with the sharp eyes that could eat us raw. We silently concentrated on work.

'Do you two ever talk like normal people?' She asked.

'That's against the rulebook for best friends,' Vihaan spoke.

'If we'll talk like normal people, then who will consider us best friends? I said after, and we high-fived.

'We are not boring like you,' Vihaan teased her.

'Excuse me?' Hiya, who suddenly felt offended, raised her voice.

'I mean, you don't speak much, that's why,' afraid of her face, Vihaan clarified.

'You can't say a person is boring because she or he is silent around you,' Hiya said. 'Just because your interests don't match mine doesn't mean I am boring.'

Vihaan apologised quickly. When we were done preparing the clay figures, Vihaan left saying he had a dinner plan with family.

No one was in the room. I got my chance. 'What are you doing tomorrow morning?' I asked Hiya.

'Why?' She asked, looking at me.

'Just wanted to know if you're available tomorrow morning?' I said.

'Well, I don't have specific plans for tomorrow.'

'Great!' I said it with joy. 'Remember about the order you've to follow?'

'That wasn't a win.'

'Yes, it was… and you lost,' I said.

'But what does it have to do with tomorrow morning?' She asked.

I took a deep breath. I was afraid of how she would react. 'A small trip on one of the nearby beaches tomorrow, you, me, and our furry tails.'

She was looking at me with a tiny grin on her face. 'Which beach?'

'Dumas beach?' I suggested.

'That's a haunted place, I've heard.'

'What about the historical beach, which was the ultimate destination of the popular Salt March?'

She chuckled. 'You mean to say *Dandi Beach?*' I was expecting an answer instead.

'Clever girl.' I patted her shoulder.

We put the model in one corner before leaving.

'My phone!' She checked her pocket while waiting for the lift. 'Wait for me.' She rushed inside. I waited for her. *Am I pressuring her? I can't force her. I must clear these things.*

'Hey, it's fine if you don't want to come. No pressure,' I said. 'I don't want you to…'

'Arnav…' She stopped me. 'I will come.'

A broad smile enlightened my face. 'I'll pick you up tomorrow morning. Be ready.'

Hiya

I woke up before the sun. My father, who usually wakes up earlier than me, looked twice to make sure he saw me. 'What circumstances forced the sun to change directions?' He mocked.

'I am going out with my friends.' I didn't want to lie, but I was also afraid of telling the truth.

'At this time? It's just 7:30.'

'Yes, I am leaving. Bye.' I ran away but then I realised that I forgot to take Doodle with me, who was chilling in my room alone. I ran again and took the stairs avoiding eye contact and brought him with me. I tried my best to not get caught.

'Where are you taking Doodle?' My father asked.

'He is coming with me, Pa.' I said. 'He really needs some fresh air.'

'You're sometimes as crazy as your mother.'

I ran before he could ask more difficult questions. Arnav was already at the society gate, waiting for me. He was strolling with his dog near his sedan car.

'I thought you're going to cancel the plan,' he said.

'No, why would I?' My Doodle was giving a friendly gesture towards Cookie by wagging his tail vigorously. Cookie was shy at first, but then she accompanied Doodle.

'Enough acquaintances. We shall move now.' Arnav grasped the leash.

'Did your parents ask you anything?' He asked.

'Yes and I said that I am going out with my friends.'

'What if he finds out you were with me only?'

'Only you know that I am here with you, so who'll tell him?'

'You daring power shocks me sometimes!'

'I know. It's just that only a few times I get to show off my skills.' Doodle kept annoying me from the backseat. Once, a strand of my hair twisted in his sharp foot nails. I made him sit down after getting my hair back successfully. We reached our destination in half an hour.

We saw an iron gate that was an entry for tourists, and no vehicles were allowed from that point. 'Can we cross the gate?' I asked.

'I don't know, but it seems like the gate is open just for us,' he said so and drove the car inside.

'No. We should go back, if someone will see us…' I saw two shopkeepers watching us like we were some celebrities who got permission to enter with our four-wheeler. 'I hope they don't call the police,' I said, reading the shopkeepers faces.

'Don't worry. We'll go together to the jail.' Arnav laughed.

He drove the car down the slope, and there, in front of us, was the wide sea as far as we could see. I'd been to this beach many times since childhood but never made an entry onto the beach in a car. He gave me tour of the beach, sitting in the car. The view was magnificent. It was neither a sunrise nor a sunset. It was just the sea… wide, serene sea and us. Very few people I saw on the beach doing exercise.

We removed our shoes in the car. He opened the back door and let both dogs roam freely on the empty beach. I put my bare feet on the cold sand. We walked till the line of the waves touching the shore.

'Would you like to avail the experience of infusing your feet in the water of the great Arabian Sea?' He asked, grasping my hand tightly and dragged me a few steps closer to the waves.

'Do you know swimming?' He asked. I denied. 'Me neither.' He laughed out loud.

Every time the waves were coming back and forth, it damped my jeans an inch more, and I wheld him tighter to avoid slipping.

'Have you ever been to this beach in the morning?' He asked

'I don't remember visiting any beaches in the morning,' I replied.

'I like it more in the morning. You know… this calm atmosphere makes me happy. I can hear the voices of the waves clearly. It's not possible in the evening because it's too crowded.'

'You can enjoy the spellbinding view of the sun meeting the sea only in the evening, right?' I added.

'Yeah, that's true,' he said.

Arnav was hungry, and there were only two shops open. Doodle and Cookie weren't in the mood to come. We both chased the leash of our respective dogs, which turned out to be a light exercise. The shop owners had corn, sugar cane juice, potato fritters, and a chain of chip packets hanging.

'Boiled corn.' We pronounced it together.

The owner served the corn on peeled leaves. We walked down the slope, eating, and sat on the bonnet of the car. It was parked at a safe distance from the shore. We sat there for a while in silence. I noticed Arnav was eating like me, neatly finishing corn rows one after another.

'Just met and are already best friends, aren't they?' Arnav said, looking at our dogs playing cheerfully, jumping, and chasing.

'These species don't really need time to know each other, unlike us.'

'I think they like each other. You know… opposites attract.' His words caught my attention. 'I mean enjoying each other's company.'

The next moment, his phone rang. He talked about his studies with someone. I continued eating corn, enjoying the early morning breeze.

'My free day is over,' he said after he shut the call. 'I have a lot of work to finish. I feel like I need forty eight hours a day.'

'You need any help?' I asked. 'I can assist you in drawing sheets. I have helped Rahul many times.'

'Rahul… Who?' He asked, curiously.

'My friend from college. He helps me with the structure, and I complete his tutorials and drawings.'

'That's… nice,' he said after a few seconds. 'What's your plan after finishing bachelors?'

'I am not sure whether to do a job or apply for post-graduation.'

'Well, I am going to apply for further studies surely,' he said, putting aside the cob.

'It's good that you're very focused on what you want to do,' I said. We watched our dogs, who were having the best time of their life.

'You know, Hiya… it's astonishing to me that we studied for twelve years together but never talked,' he said, looking at me.

'And look at us today,' I said, adjusting my flying hair. 'I never thought I would be sitting on the beach alone with you, talking about life,' I added.

'Me neither,' he said, chuckling. 'You're a very good person, Hiya, and a good friend.'

I smiled back without answering. The sun was getting hotter the more it was ascending in the sky.

'I think it is time to pack our dogs in the car again,' he said.

'I don't think it's going to be easy.' I jumped off the bonnet, and we ran to chase our dogs.

Arnav

'If I ask you to keep this as our little secret, will you keep it?' I asked her in the car while returning back home.

'What secret?' She asked, cleaning sand from her feet.

She didn't get my point about what I was trying to say to her. She looked at me for clarification.

'Don't tell Vihaan about our trip, and I want you to keep it a secret,' I explained.

She was confused. 'Is there any problem?'

'No nothing. Just say that you won't tell,' I told her before she could make things difficult for me to explain.

She finally agreed. She must have had a thought about keeping a secret from my best friend. I had no choice. He would have started giving me lectures. On the other note, I don't think Hiya thinks of me that way. *Maybe she likes Rahul, her friend from college.*

'Your offer of help was genuine, or was it a joke?' I asked, concentrating on driving.

'I gave you a real deal.'

'What are your charges per sheet, mam?' I scoffed.

'It's free of charge.' She crossed her hands and smiled. 'Bring your work to class. I'll take it with me and give it back to you tomorrow.'

'No, I can't take that risk. One wrong line, and my sheet will be thrown into the garbage,' I said.

'Then how do you want me to help you?'

'Come to my house if it's ok for you.'

'Your house?' She made a face like I'd said something unexpected.

She nodded after releasing herself from mute mode. I dropped her at the gate of her society. I was smiling for no reason, looking at her, walking with her dog. Cookie desperately wanted to come on board. She jumped up and took the seat next to me.

* * *

The doorbell rang. I rushed to open it, but my mother had already unlocked the door.

'That's Hiya, my friend,' I said to my mother.

'Oh, I've never seen you before,' my mother replied, welcoming Hiya.

I could see the awkwardness on Hiya's face and pursed my lips to hide my laugh.

'Ma… She is here to help,' I said. 'Architectural stuff.'

My mother looked at me strangely. That was the first time a girl knocked on my door. Most of the time, it's Vihaan or my other boys who come to my place. My mother offered Hiya a glass of water to drink. She talked with her for a while and then went to her room, leaving us behind. To avoid the strange silence between me and Hiya, I showed her the way to my room. Her eyes took a tour of my room, which I had just cleaned before her arrival. She praised some of the drawings I had displayed on my study desk. Seeing Hiya in the room, Cookie didn't bark. My mother showed up after a while. I saw her dressed up and asked the reason.

'The ladies group of the apartment is going to *Dandi* beach,' she replied.

I and Hiya looked at each other as we heard the word *Dandi*. There were plenty of chances of getting caught if I had planned my visit in the evening. I followed my mother from my room to the hall. 'Is she studying with you in college?' Ma asked.

'She was in school with me.'

'I never noticed or heard of her when you were in school,' she said.

'I am wondering the same thing.' I murmured. My mother didn't hear me as one lady from her group knocked on the door and told her to come as it was getting late. After she left, I closed the door and ran back to my room. I saw Hiya reading something from a paper she was holding.

'What are you so afraid of,' she read aloud the lines.

I never liked someone touching my personal things. It made me uncomfortable. I took that paper from her hand.

'You wrote it?' She asked. 'I never knew you like to write.'

'It's unfinished.' I put the paper in my drawer and closed it. 'I was writing it for me.'

'I also write sometimes,' she said. 'Not poems, but life incidents that happen to me.'

'Really! I also thought of writing but was unable to do so.' My discomfort vanished magically after listening to her. 'My busy life is not giving me chances to pen down my journey.'

'In that case, I'd like to read the entire thing. Finish it fast,' she commanded.

'I'll try my best.'

I gave her all the required tools and explained the drawings in detail. She had good knowledge of reading plans. She spread the white sheet on the floor. I sat next to her with my sheet.

I discussed my way of drawing and shared my tips for error free outputs. She was a quick learner and started working. Her speed of drawing was good enough. I wondered how many times she would have helped Rahul, her friend from college, which made her work like a pro. She was working on drawings more seriously than me. She asked about her doubts in between. I finished my sheet first and sat next to Hiya. I offered my help, but she denied as if it was her personal work, and she knew it better. After two hours, she showed me her work. I examined it and corrected the errors.

'Are you a tea or coffee person?' I asked, putting all the stuff back in its place.

'If it's tea, I like it hot, and if it's coffee, I like it cold,' she replied.

'Great. I'll make cold coffee for us,' I said. 'I make the world's best cold coffee.'

I didn't allow her in the kitchen as my recipe was a secret. I let her to play with Cookie in the living room. I prepared the coffee and presented it to her. My eyes waited for her reaction as she took the first sip.

'This is really good.' She praised. 'Seriously, who taught you?'

'This is my own recipe.' I clinked my glass with hers.

'Can I know it?' She asked enthusiastically.

'At no cost I'll reveal my secret ingredient.' I smiled.

* * *

Everyone was busy working on their models. The list contained a total of ten entries. I and Hiya were working on the final details. Naveen was on a round to check everyone's work. He wasn't just inspecting but also guiding and sharing tips with everyone. He was happy to see the progress of our model. He asked us to revise the software tools he taught us in the last lecture. Instead of obeying Naveen's command, we decided to watch all the models. I and Hiya realised that the competition was tough and we had a very low chance of winning.

'I wish Vihaan was here to check all the models,' Hiya said.

Her words reminded me about Vihaan's meeting with her sister's boyfriend. I completely forgot to ask him about that. *I hope he didn't make it hard for her sister. She is a nice person, and I am sure she must have chosen a good match for her.* Before I could take out my phone to get an update from Vihaan, Naveen made an announcement of the final presentation date of the contest, which was December 17.

'No, not that day!' I mumbled and frowned. Hiya heard me. 'It's my birthday,' I went closer to her ear and said. I saw an excitement in her eyes.

Naveen called all the participants to explain how to take pictures of the scenes. How the video will be made. Later, he came to conduct the class, which felt boring in front of all the new work that was assigned to us. I discussed with Hiya how we'd shoot the pictures. She shared the same energy as me during the discussion. Her way of thinking and many of her hobbies were the same as mine, and that's why I always felt so comfortable talking with her.

'You've any special plans for your birthday?' Hiya asked, coming out from the class.

'No, nothing but it's me who should decide what I want to do on my birthday, to sleep all day in bed or to have a party with friends,' I said, complaining. 'But when there's an alternate plan written for you by destiny, you can't escape.'

'True that. I spent my birthday this year with test paper and answer sheets, against my will,' she expressed. 'Had no choice.'

'What's your date and month?'

'It's May 26.'

I shook my head. 'Anyways, I have an offer for you as a token of your help.'

She helped me with my drawing sheet, which saved me two hours. She deserved a reward for that.

'What do you want to eat? I'll take you there.'

'Not required.'

'No, you'll have to eat at least one of your favourite food dishes,' I requested.

She looked around and pointed her finger. 'There.' I looked in that direction. It was a small stall of *panipuri*, on the other side of the road. I was amazed by her choice.

'Is that what you want? Really?'

She nodded and smiled. We crossed the road and reached near the stall.

'Think once again. You can ask for something better and more expensive,' I said before ordering.

'It's all I want!' She giggled.

Hiya

My life, most of the time, is a struggle between wanting to do something but having no idea how to do it by avoiding possible human interaction. I feel immensely grateful to be born in an era where free messaging apps are at the service of people like me.

'Do you think that I should call?' I asked Doodle for expert advice, but he was as clueless as me. I was holding my phone, ready to hit the call button at 12:00am on December 17. Before I could come to a conclusion, my friends began showering wishes on Arnav in the group. I tapped the back button continuously until I saw my home screen.

What am I even thinking? He must be busy attending to the calls of people closer to him. I thumped my phone on the bed and grabbed my book to read. *But I should at least send a text to him. That won't look odd.* I put my book aside and stretched myself to pick up the phone.

'Happy Birthday, Arnav. Enjoy your day!' I sent my wish. There were no reply from Arnav expressing his gratitude. *Is he too busy to check his phone for just a half-minute?*

I searched for my phone first thing in the morning to check the messages. Arnav was still missing. His last seen status was hidden. Later, when I was in college, he finally replied to each and every birthday wish, including mine. I thought everyone in the group would start debating over Arnav, but nothing like I imagined happened.

Boys & girls, December 20, Sunday, my house, pizza party. Don't miss it! Arnav sent the message on the group in the late evening.

Oh bhaii, why not. Anytime ready for pizza! I am in.

True… no denials for pizza, long live bro!

I am in. Thanks in advance Arnav.

Hanji, Will come.

I'm glad that you're part of the group, and will be there for sure.

Everyone replied to Arnav's invitation.

It's a good feat to feed hungry stomachs, and we are forever hungry. Always positive for pizza, brother! Vihaan accepted the invitation. Only I was left to answer. After rewriting the message for the fifth time, I texted, *Yes, sure.*

As there were three teams that were not presentation-ready, the final competition date was postponed. When Arnav came to know about it, he felt overjoyed. He had an important submission on the same day. With that, it wouldn't have been possible to attend the final competition for him. I was glad that he invited me to his birthday party.

It wasn't really hard this time to find Arnav's home. I wore a mustard-yellow tunic with blue jeans. Kavya and I knocked on the door together. Arnav welcomed us warmly. He was wearing a simple grey shirt and black jeans. The woody perfume smell coming out of him was so good. Everyone whom Arnav invited was present, except Vihaan. Cookie came running towards me. I rubbed her head. She sniffed and licked my hand. Arnav's mother came out from the kitchen. She saw me and smiled. She questioned Vihaan's absence.

'If he had come by now, Cookie wouldn't be roaming freely.' Arnav giggled.

The doorbell rang. 'That's Vihaan for sure.' Arnav rushed to his room with Cookie. His mother opened the door. Vihaan had brought a cake. He entered singing a happy birthday song.

'I told you not to bring anything and come with an empty stomach,' Arnav said, coming out of the room.

'My stomach is empty and before pizzas arrive, let's have a piece of cake first.'

Arnav led us all to the terrace as he had made arrangements there. Visiting the terrace has been my favourite hobby, and I get excited without any reason. Arnav's building had 8 floors. The terrace door was locked.

'Why do they lock it? I am sure there is nothing to steal,' Vihaan said.

'Just in case child like you might jump to measure the height of this building, that's why!' Arnav mocked. He had the key and unlocked it. The cool breeze of December embraced us when Arnav pushed the door.

'Whoa! That's the first time I am witnessing such a lovely view of our city.' Nikhil expanded his hands in the air.

'Me too.' I whispered. No one heard me. The view was indeed great. Each direction was begging for attention. I couldn't decide which direction had the best view. I stood near the parapet wall, bent over, and looked down to see the ground level. My scooter looked like the size of an ant from the terrace. I and Kavya set the mat on the floor. Vihaan placed the cake in the centre and called everyone.

'Don't sing the song please. It's…'

'Happy birthday to you… Happy birthday to Arniii.' Vihaan started singing the very next second, dramatically loudly. Everyone followed Vihaan's lines and clapped until Arnav cut the cake and stuffed a piece in everyone's mouth. He overloaded Vihaan's mouth with cake as revenge. After much debate over a pizza menu, Arnav ordered four different large pizzas and stuffed garlic breads. Arnav had forgot to bring the coke bottles from home and was requesting Vihaan, who clearly said, 'You're the host. You go and bring'. We were all enjoying their little war. They kept passing the responsibility. At last, I and Kavya went to bring it. Suchi joined us, too.

The door was open, but I still chose to ring the doorbell. I asked for the coke bottles when I saw Arnav's mother. Kavya and Suchi went to the washroom. Aunty asked me to wait till she searched for the plastic cups. There was a mouth-watering smell of *dal tadka* coming from the kitchen. I heard the noise of a vessel colliding. I saw aunty standing on a small stool, trying to grab something from one of the wall cabinets.

'May I help you, aunty?' I asked.

'Yes dear, can you hold this please?' She gave me a bunch of steel bowls. She pulled out a chain of plastic cups. I couldn't stop myself from praising the smell of *dal tadka*. She poured some in one small bowl and gave it to me. I took a spoonful and blew air, as it was smoking hot. It was really delicious and tasted exactly like my mother's recipe.

'You know cooking?' She asked me after I appreciated the taste.

'Not much, but yes, I help my mother in the kitchen.'

'That's good,' she said. 'I tell my son to learn at least the basics of food, but he always has a reason to avoid it.'

I laughed and imagined Arnav putting his best efforts into cooking in the same kitchen. It turned horrible when I imagined him blowing up the kitchen. Though his son is an excellent cold coffee maker. I wanted to say it but Kavya and Suchi appeared in the kitchen. They had taken a one-one bottle of coke with them.

'Take Cookie with you. I am going out for a walk and Arnav's father will come late,' aunty said to us.

All the boys had climbed up on the masonry water tank. Scared Vihaan, shouted from up to take Cookie back. Arnav came down, took the leash from my hand, and tied it to the wall in the corner.

'Want to come up?' Arnav asked us. 'The view is great.'

'I want to come.' I said, excitedly. Kavya joined me.

The wooden ladder wasn't in good condition and looked risky as two steps were missing. Kavya dared to climb first. Arnav held the ladder tightly till we reached the top. Nikhil extended his hand of help on the other side. The place where I was standing seemed riskier than the ladder. It had no railings or walls of protection.

In a small place, we all stood, shoulders colliding with each other. But the view was great and I could see entire town. Vihaan took photographs and selfies of us. Tiny street lights were illuminating one by one as the world around us was turning into night. People living in high-rise buildings have the advantage of an astonishing view. I would've come to the terrace daily if I was living in this apartment. When the people of the world fight with their chaos on the ground, terraces will always be there to calm you down, to take all your worries away, and to make you realise how small your problems are in front of this big fat universe.

We all came down when the pizzas arrived, Arnav sent Vihaan and Nikhil to collect. I saw Cookie sitting alone, getting bored and went to check upon her. I played with her for a while.

'Take her home tonight with you,' Arnav said.

'I won't mind if you allow it.' I smiled.

'I wanted to show you something.' He came closer, bent down and said to me, 'I'll show you before you leave,' he said looking around, in case someone might be listening.

What does he have to show? What that subject could be? Were there any communications that were left in the middle? Was I in trouble? Have I done something wrong in the sheet? He could have possibly faced rejection because of any of my stupid mistakes. Before the coil of my thoughts could get more space to expand, the pizza boys brought pizzas.

'Dig in,' Arnav said, and we started with peppy paneer.

'To Arnav!' Vihaan raised a slice of pizza. We all raised our slices.

I didn't know about Arnav, but his birthday surely became memorable to me. Maybe a lifetime treasure!

Arnav

'Hey, how long has it been since we went on a trip?' Jhanvi asked, eating pizza. 'We should plan something.'

'Remember, our last trip to Diu?' Jay exclaimed. 'It was fun.'

I wasn't part of that trip, as I had gone to Shimla and Manali with my parents. Vihaan mentioned his fight with one completely stoned person. He would have ended up in jail if Nikhil hadn't arrived on time. Anjali recalled the incident where she lost her phone and later found it deeply buried in her backpack. Only I, Hiya, and Kavya were not a part of that trip. We had no other option except to listen to everyone. I looked at Hiya, a few of her hair strands fluttering in the cold air, sitting right in front of me, listening and smiling over Diu stories.

I checked my pocket to confirm I still had what I wanted to show. *Is it a good idea? How will she react? Will she respect me or just laugh it out?* I thought looking at her sweet smiley face. Everyone was busy suggesting a place where we could go next. I refused again to join and they all threw their anger on me.

'I know why he is saying no.' Vihaan came to my defence. He gave me a look and said 'The semester's ending soon so can't plan right now.'

'Yeah right, I forgot that I have exams to attend,' Drishti spoke sadly.

'We'll visit *Saputara* in monsoon!' Vihaan declared.

We continued discussing places until we ran out of place names. The pizza boxes were empty, and our stomachs were full. All my friends started leaving one by one. Kavya asked Hiya to go. She looked at me. *How am I supposed to talk with her to say don't go?*

Vihaan came forward and hugged me. 'Thanks for the treat Arnii, I hope you get what you want in life.' The seriousness in his voice forced me to tighten my grip over him.

I released Cookie once Vihaan left. Kavya expressed her gratitude and was preparing to leave. Hiya's facial expressions were saying that she didn't want to go. I was still in need of a good valid excuse to stop her. When the lift stopped on the fifth floor, I dropped my hopes there.

'How was your submission?' Hiya asked all of a sudden. My speedster mind found the excuse in her question.

'Good that you reminded me Hiya. If you don't mind, will you give me a few minutes?' I said holding the lift door. *I hope she gets my hint and lets Kavya go alone.* I said to myself. Hiya came out from the lift. We both looked at Kavya. *Please go kavya, leave us alone.* I screamed in my mind.

'I've to reach home. I'll take leave,' Kavya said. That brought a grin to my face.

'Yeah sure, I don't want to waste your time,' I said in over-excitement.

Hiya looked at me once the lift took Kavya down.

'Was that an intentional question?' I asked her. She was clueless.

'No, I asked as I recalled,' she said once she got my point. *She is way too innocent and honest.*

'If you don't mind, can we go back to the terrace?' I asked hesitantly. 'My parents are at home.'

'I love to visit those places again and again which brings peace to my soul,' she replied.

We went to the terrace again. I pulled out the paper from my pocket. 'Read this and tell me how it is.' I ran to turn on one and only tube light. She opened the paper. 'Oh, you completed it!'

'I am no poet but I tried my best,' I said and asked her to read loudly.

What are you so afraid of?

When you're aware of your abilities.

What are you so scared of?

When you know your weaknesses.

You cannot be that fragile or vulnerable,

An introduction of your strength is unknown to your struggle.

Just give it a thought dear,

Follow your heart above all your fears.

There will be haters, there will be lovers.

There will be discouragers, there will be admires.

There will be challengers, there will be supporters.

There will be betrayers, there will be saviours.

On the path, you will be hurt, heartbroken, devastated,

But someone will be there to support you against all barricades.

The day you'll reach the desired height of success,

The whole world will come forward to appreciate.

Tell them to buckle up the seat-belts of their chair,

The unsung story of your success is yet to be shared.'

She stared at the paper for a while and then folded it back.

'You like it?' I asked, enthusiastic. 'Be honest, please.'

'You should frame this in your room so that you'll feel inspired every day.' She grinned. 'This is very encouraging and beautiful.'

'Thanks for the compliment!' I said happily and took the paper back.

'Why me?' she asked after a short pause.

'Sorry?' I was processing the thought that she liked my attempt.

'Why did you choose me to show instead of… someone closer to you?' The way she looked into my eyes, I forgot what to say. I struggled to make eye contact.

'You're not bound to answer,' she politely said, maybe reading my anxiety.

'No… it's just that it was you who saw this first and I…'

'Why not Vihaan?' She asked. Her questions were becoming tougher than my exams. Now I wanted her to leave before I could drain myself completely into embarrassment.

'I honestly have no answer.' I released a fake laugh at the end.

We looked at each other. 'I'll leave now,' she said. Her feet weren't moving. I took a step forward and hugged her gently. 'Thanks for coming!'

I gazed at her till she disappeared. Cookie tried to follow her but I stopped. I pulled out my paper and read it again. I searched for the answer she expected from me. It's just that she was the one who encouraged me to write and when I submitted my assignment, she asked *why! I mean why? What nonsense question that she was seeking an answer from me?*

Vihaan

'A month!' I said, shockingly. I got disappointed when I heard from Arnav that he wasn't going to come anytime soon as he had more important things to focus on in college.

'Or may be more than that.' He pulled out two shirts from his wardrobe and put them in his bag. 'Maa, where are my shirts that you took for ironing?' He shouted.

There was a tech-fest in Arnav's college then he had exams to attend and moreover his department was planning a study tour so he was busier than any other human on the planet. Aunty brought a stack of neatly pressed shirts.

'I've prepared tea for you both. Have it before you go.'

'Sure. I'll have some snacks too,' I said following her footsteps.

I, Arnav and his parents were sipping tea over the round dining table. Arnav's Cookie was tied in the balcony. She was barking at the street dogs that were fighting and howling. Uncle asked us about our future plans.

'That girl who came to help you with your sheets, is she studying architecture?' Aunty questioned Arnav. It confused me.

'Girl, who?' I looked at Arnav and asked. There was a prompt change in his facial expression. 'Am I missing something… Arnav?' I asked suspiciously.

'She was at the party too, that day. I forgot her name,' aunty said.

'She doesn't study with me ma, I told you before.' Arnav looked more irritated. 'She was in school with me.'

Arnav's face clearly told me that something was there of which I was completely unknown. Being unaware of the incident happening in the person's life, whom I call my best friend, and the one who shared every little thing since childhood, didn't give me good vibes. If my instincts were correct, the name Arnav's mother was struggling to recall was on my tongue. Arnav, who couldn't make eye contact with me, was the proof that I was right.

'Hiya… came to help,' he finally spilled the words. I talked through my eyes. 'She wanted to help. The day when you were absent, we had a small discussion regarding studies.'

'Oh, so that's why,' I said dramatically.

'Yes, Hiya, that's a nice name. I wonder what does that means,' aunty said, sipping tea.

'Yeah… nice name indeed.' I said, staring at Arnav. 'The meaning of the name Hiya is *heart.*'

Arnav looked at me sharply.

'That girl indeed seems like a person with a good heart.' Aunty stood up, collected the empty crockeries from the table and took it to the kitchen.

* * *

'What was that?' Arnav asked, irritated when we came out of his house. 'What are you trying to prove?'

'Nothing,' I said, madly. 'In fact, I should ask you the same.'

Arnav went numb for a while. 'Look… It's not what you think. That path is not for me,' he said, pacifically.

'What if Hiya starts walking on that path you're creating?' I argued tensely.

'Are you speaking with your senses alive, Vihaan?' Arnav ruffled. 'Why would she think of me? I am sure she has more important things to do than that.'

'I know, but… the way she looks at you, man!'

Arnav rolled his eyes and sighed. 'For God's sake, please. She is a friend of mine, and I am hers. That's it.' He retorted.

'Do you think I'm using my own words?'

'Yes!' He said, annoyingly. 'I mean, is that what you think for me and her?'

'It's not me, Arnav! It's you who is giving me plenty of reasons to think.' I argued loudly. He took the key from my hand to ignite the bike engine. I sat behind him.

'Trust me, Vihaan, you'll be the first person to know about the girl with whom I'll decide to be with,' Arnav said.

'I do. But your actions are different from what you're insisting to believe with your words,' I said. 'For your record,

Hiya doesn't seem like a girl who would visit any random boy's house like this to help, including yours and mine.'

My words might have influenced him, as he didn't say a word on the way. *Did I speak too much?* I thought. He was murmuring a song all the way. Hiya was already present. She waved her hand, looking at us. I responded quickly, but Arnav didn't. *I guess I went too far. I've known Arnav more than Hiya. I believe he honestly wasn't looking at Hiya the way I was thinking. I must not create false rumours. Never in my wildest dreams did I imagine creating a conflict between them. I think I should put an end to my fairy tale.* But a part of my heart really believed in the story of these two sweet dog lovers.

Observing his reaction, I thought that he would not take the seat next to Hiya, but he sat next to her and greeted her as usual. In no time, my thoughts took a U turn, and I began imagining stories again. Hiya gave us an update on all the models that were shifted to the next room. Arnav wanted to know the new date for finals.

'Why would you care? You've decided to leave us already,' I stated.

'Leave?' Hiya was confused.

'Oh, you don't know yet! He's leaving us.' I read her face. She was more worried than she should be.

'Stop spreading rumours, Vihaan.' Arnav said coldly. He seemed still upset with me. 'I am taking a short break. College is my first priority.'

'It should be,' I said. He gave me a grumpy look. I was smiling under my lips.

'I was thinking of taking a break too,' Hiya said. 'For exams.'

'If all my team members are taking a break, then I should too.' I declared. 'I'll check on Naveen if he's free then we can talk.'

Hiya

Exams should be banned in the cold season so that we, the student community, can sleep peacefully. I was running late, rushing here and there in my room to collect the necessary things for my exam. I was reading until three in the morning and turned off the alarm that tried to wake me up. My mother was getting worried about what I'd write in my exam. I packed my bag. Doodle, who came from his morning walk with my father, got excited as usual, as if seeing me for the first time in many years. It was hard to get rid of him, but I managed.

I found my exam room and saw my classmates there, heads dipped in the books. When the bell rang, we took our seats. I got the paper in my hand, it looked easy to me. I finished it before time.

'Let's go somewhere once exams are over!' Priya exclaimed, when we were in the canteen.

'We've been saying this to each other since the beginning of this semester. Try something else.' Rahul interrupted.

'I know. But we've got just roughly one year now & then we'll all be separated.' Priya said unhappily.

The word *separation* triggered me. It put me in a chain of thoughts, and it was more and more engrossing. All the debates in mind were for only one person, Arnav. *Will I ever be seeing him again? Will I ever meet him in my life? In maybe two or three months, my classes will be over. What if he comes back after two months or maybe three? I'll never get to see him then!*

Priya jerked my shoulder to bring me back to reality.

'Our life will change once we step out of this college,' I said, taking a bite of a sandwich.

'Sometimes I wonder if the earth is spinning fast or is it us expecting it to slow down,' Rahul said sadly.

'Let's just not think about all these things right now and focus on this sandwich,' I said and stuffed a bite in my mouth.

I saw Kavya with her classmates entering the canteen. She saw me and I waved my hand. She came to me asking about my exams. We chatted for a while then she went back to join her classmates.

'You never said that you've a friend in computer science!' Rahul expressed with eagerness.

'Someone is desperate to talk with the girls of the CS department,' Priya said. We both laughed.

'Choices are more than what I've got from my department,' he said.

'You can't say that in-front of us, Rahul. That's rude.' Priya roared.

'Can you share her phone number?' He asked me.

'No way. She will kill me.'

'Do you have the number of the girl sitting next to her?' I looked and denied.

'Now you know why I am asking for your friend's number?'

'I'll ask Kavya first,' I replied. 'If she says yes then only I'll share her number.'

* * *

A group of twenty people, including me, went to the *Dandi* beach after exams got over. The sun was so hot that it felt like summer came early. We were all sitting in a garden surrounded by large trees. We ate snacks and then rushed to the beach. I sat on the shore with a few others. I recalled all the memories I shared with Arnav that I enjoyed on the same beach. Isn't it amazing that you have different memories with different people attached to the same place? Doodle enjoys beaches more than me, and I never realised it until I brought him to the place.

I should thank Arnav for that. But how will I say it if I never see him again? Why does it feel too odd to think that the chances of seeing him again are slim? Maybe I'll see him whenever there's a reunion. I must keep my hopes high.

One of my friends from the group dragged me and Priya into the sea. The amount of pictures we all clicked that day was more than we took in the last three years. Half of our clothes were wet. Two of us accidentally fell in the water and got completely wet. We spent the entire evening there. We lived it like that was the last time we were enjoying it together.

Vihaan

Ma summoned us for dinner. She placed a bowl of *palak paneer* on the table. I and Risha decorated the table with dishes and glasses.

'Now that you've only a year remaining, what are your plans next?' My father asked.

'What do you suggest?' I asked.

'You can join me, see how things work and make your decision accordingly.'

Since the day I made up my decision to become civil engineer, I wanted to work with my father and he was giving me a chance. 'Sure, we can discuss that once I finish my study,' I replied.

'What about you Risha? Do you want to join me too or want to apply for other roles?' My father asked my sister.

He was in the mood to set their children's careers on the spot. He never asks such serious questions daily or weekly but whenever the discussions start, it can go up to an hour.

'Our relatives have started asking for Risha... about marriage.' My mother disturbed the ongoing father-daughter conversation.

I and Risha both looked at each other. Risha opposed it instantly. Ma pacified her and assured her that they won't do anything without her permission.

'Let her do what she wants to do,' my father said. 'You want to become a professor, go ahead.'

The discussion went on for a few more minutes. It turned from serious topics to funny ones. I was sure about what was going on in Risha's mind, and for expert advice, I knew she would knock on my door, and I heard it at eleven in the night. She showed me a container of ice cream. We finished half of the ice cream silently. I was waiting for her to start.

'What am I supposed to do?' She let out her anxiety.

'Is my brother-in-law ready for marriage?' I asked, licking the ice cream off the spoon.

'No, of course not and neither am I.'

'Then follow father's advice, earn money, live your life.'

She discussed her plans and plots for how she can introduce her boyfriend. Some of them were really idiotic, which forced me to wonder how someone could fall for such a stoop level of intelligence. We emptied the ice cream container but couldn't finalise the perfect plan. Later, I had to throw her out of the room as her words were becoming intolerable.

* * *

I met Hiya after two weeks. She was talking with Naveen. He saw me and welcomed me with a handshake. He was happy to see us after a short break. He asked about Arnav but his break wasn't over yet. The new final date was released and Naveen asked us all to be present. In addition, there was a small party, too.

'When Arnav is coming back?' Hiya asked.

There was a curiosity in her eyes, I could clearly see. I had the answer in my mouth but I denied and suggested she ask him.

'Me?' She was shocked as if I told her to visit Arnav's home to know.

She didn't ask though. She made an excuse and moved to her computer as Naveen came to teach.

* * *

'I am super hungry,' I said. 'Let's go to the Phoenix Cafe afterwards.'

I had questions in my fickle mind dancing ever since the seeds *'Hiya & Arnav'* were sowed. I wanted to clear a few things from my thoughts and this was the best chance to do it in Arnav's absence.

'What's going on in your life, Hiya?' I asked her in the cafe.

'Nothing, just clearing semesters to get my Bachelor's degree.'

'That's it? Nothing controversial?' I asked, suspiciously. 'Who am I asking though, the most sincere and obedient girl!'

She laughed it out too. 'It's all assumptions that people make and believe in without knowing me or talking to me.'

'Is it?' I said. She nodded. 'Then tell me something that can change my assumptions.'

She wore silence with her contagious smile. The waiter served a plate of garlic bread for me and a chocolate milkshake for her.

'Ok. I'll speak words, answer yes if it's related to your likes and interests and no if not,' I said. 'No lies. That's the only rule.' I cleared and she agreed.

'Love Dogs?' I started

'Eternally yes.'

'Lizards?'

'No. But I want to hold an iguana.'

'Stars?'

'Yes.'

'Study?'

'Not much.'

'Have Dreams?'

'Yes.'

'Morning person?'

'No, night owl.'

'Momos?'

'No. Terrible taste.'

'That's rude. I love momos. Sports bike?'

'No.'

'Have cheated on someone?'

'No.'

'Have copied in exams?'

'Yes.'

'Unbelievable! Boys as friends?'

'Yes.'

'Have a crush on someone?'

'Yes.'

'Is that Arnav?'

'Yes.'

'Checkmate!' I knocked my fist on the table.

'No. I just said yes in the flow. I didn't realise your question.'

'Don't justify, Hiya. The beans have spilled already.' I said. She looked terribly confused and worried. She was desperately trying to change my mind. I held both her hands. 'Say the truth. You've got feelings for him or not?' I could see the suffering on her face, like her deep, dark secret was revealed against her will.

'Say yes or no, nothing else.' I tightened my grip when she attempted to release herself. She looked in my eyes for a while. I raised my eyebrow for her answer.

She shook her head gently. 'I knew it.' I leaned on my seat. She abruptly left with an angry face. I ran to stop her, my leg got twisted and I fell on the ground. I woke up from my sleep. It was a heart-breaking realisation that I dreamt the whole cafeteria scene.

How can I have a dream like this? I splashed water on my face. *Stop playing the role of cupid, no one asked for your advice or your opinion. Live and let live.*

For the next two days, I couldn't concentrate and was unable to understand *why I was being a leader here and why I couldn't mind my own business. I should find a girlfriend for me instead of digging into other people's personal lives.* Two sides of my mind were at war. One wanted to investigate, and the other wanted to pack up and leave. To figure it out, I had to give myself one last chance to satisfy my soul.

Hiya

I would have run away if I had the chance to do so. The sudden ache in my heart and the way my fingers went cold. The ground beneath my feet had moved away. I was transported to a different world with completely strange feelings. It wasn't easy to remain calm and act like it didn't affect me. The acceptance of Vihaan's words wasn't easy. Handling the racing heartbeat wasn't easy. The fact that talking to Arnav will be difficult for me now that I know he already has someone in his life crushed my inner peace.

'Sorry, but I wasn't supposed to tell you this. Arnav has strictly warned me not to tell anyone about his girlfriend,' Vihaan said, staring into my eyes. I couldn't dare to look at him. If he was a good face reader, he would have noticed the change in my face and my body language.

'Please consider it a slip of the tongue,' he added later. I nodded, hardly looking at him. It became more annoying when Vihaan didn't stop trying to convince me. I left the class early. I couldn't hold back my tears while riding back home. I had no right to feel bad. *I never expressed my feelings to Arnav. I can't even consider it as a heartbreak. I wish I had told Arnav about what I feel for him.* I wanted to scream out loud with all the energy left in my body.

My father read my face and asked me the reason of my sad eyes when we were eating dinner. I told him a lie. I didn't speak much and ran to my room after putting empty plate in the sink. I locked the door and sat on the floor next to Doodle. I hugged him tightly and cried out of my heart.

Hey, coming to the class next week. You too coming right?

It's been so long. I've so much to share. Please be there.

The text messages from Arnav brought tears back to my eyes. *What did he want to share? Was he going to mention his girlfriend, her name, how beautiful she is, how they first met, how they came closer, and how they became partners?* I didn't reply to him.

I didn't want to attend the class, but I had to, as it was the final day of the competition. The room was packed with all the participants. There was no sign of Vihaan or Arnav. Naveen told all the participants to stay close to their models as the competition was to begin.

I saw our model from afar with no representative. I collided with someone on the way. I would have fallen down on the floor and everyone would have laughed, but I was saved by the same person I collided with. When I opened my eyes to look, Arnav was smiling brightly. 'Slow down.' He pulled me up and created a space to stand. It felt like I was watching him after a decade. He had grown a beard that made him look a bit unrecognisable and weird. I had to make sure it was only him. Before my thoughts could start controlling me, I turned away.

We were waiting for our turn, and there were four more groups before us. Meanwhile, both the boys were busy chatting, murmuring, and laughing. I was standing at a decent distance from them, trying to avoid every possible eye contact with Arnav. I never thought that two boys could also gossip like that. Arnav expressed enthusiastically all the incidents that happened in his college. His daily boring lectures, the tech-fest celebration, and the activities he took part in, the fun they had, and the stories continued.

When the judges came to our table, we presented our work, and they were impressed. One of them was specifically affected by the story. However, I couldn't figure out what was so impressive. The story just popped up in my mind. I didn't do any hard work for it. When the results came out, we won third place. None of us could believe but we got a small trophy and a cash prize of a thousand rupees, which we instantly decided to spend on having dinner.

* * *

While we were waiting for our food order at the cafe, Arnav began talking and this time it wasn't about his study or fest or anything else.

'Guys, this is a perfect time to announce this,' he said.

Please don't. My inner voice urged, looking at his shiny eyes. *Wait, if Vihaan has asked me to keep the secret, then why would Arnav say it out loud? If he wants to, then he would have told just me, as Vihaan already knew. Arnav probably has something else to say.*

'My college is planning an international educational trip and I am going!' He couldn't control his excitement.

'Whoa! That's amazingly amazing,' Vihaan exclaimed loudly. 'Where?'

'Dubai. It's a five day trip.'

I was more relieved that he didn't declare his girlfriend. *Will his girlfriend also join? Does she study with him? Did Vihaan mention it?* I couldn't memorise. *Hope she is not joining!*

'How many students are joining?' I asked just to assume.

'As of now twenty,' He replied. 'We still have a few more days to book the seats.'

By the time our order of pizza and cheese garlic bread came, the discussion ended there. Both the boys, without any further discussion, handed me over the trophy as the judges gave more points to the story.

'What do you think I am yours, an attendant?' Vihaan suddenly roared over a call. He stood up aggressively. 'I've to go and pick up daddy's princess, see you later,' he said and left immediately.

I and Arnav took a walk after we both felt like eating extra. 'So… What's keeping you busy these days huh?' Arnav asked. 'No reply, no other news, which world are you living in?'

'Nothing, life is keeping me busy,' I replied.

'For me also, the last month was super active. I might have lost a few kilos.'

I was more interested in gazing at him than listening to him. His face was shimmering under the street lights. I had changed my mind about his beard and he wasn't looking weird. He was looking okay and good. We walked for ten minutes. He talked about how excited he is for his trip. He also talked about his Cookie's stories that how she has become a fully grown adult and people are more afraid of her as her barking skills have gone up so impressively.

'But for me she is still my little girl, whom I can't lift more than one minute now.' He laughed. 'She is so heavy and too big to fit in my lap.' I wanted to keep walking with him, but my mind kept reminding me about his girlfriend.

Arnav

'You've your passport, visa and all documents?' My mother asked me for the sixth time.

'Yes Ma,' I said, a little annoyed.

'Don't forget to inform us once you reach there and stay with your group,' my father advised.

Apparently, I was the first one from my home to visit a place that wasn't part of my country. That was the reason for my parents' panicky behaviour. They had never been to any other country. I struggled not to be rude when both of them were offering their individual opinions and advice. I heard all the parents of my tour mates doing the same thing. At last, after listening to the list of 'dos and don'ts', I and all the other students got on the bus that took us to Mumbai International Airport. My mother couldn't hold her tears while waving her hand.

Luckily, I got a window seat in the plane. I'd never seen such an astonishing night view of Mumbai from above. Soon, the plane reached above the clouds, and there was nothing to see. When it reached its maximum height, I saw the most breathtaking full moon of my life. It seemed so close, like within a few minutes of flying, I'd be able to land on the moon. Hiya would have gone crazy if she had seen such a glorious moon. I took a few pictures, which weren't very appealing compared to what I saw with my naked eye, but I saved them for Hiya.

When the pilot made an announcement of landing, my eyes searched for the most famous landmark, the tallest man-made structure in the world, the Burj Khalifa. In between the tiny, glittering lights of the city I found the tallest tower.

Though it was an educational tour, no one cared to stick to the education. The first place we visited was the Palm *Jumeirah and* one of the praiseworthy hotels in the world, the Atlantis. After a monorail ride, we headed to the Dubai Marina. Emirates Crown, Canyon Tower, Princess Tower, Pinnacle, and the list went on. The seventy-eighty-storey skyscrapers made me realise how indigent I am and how prosperous the world is. I was so impressed by the different sizes and shapes of all the buildings there.

The next day was packed with a visit to the Dubai Museum, a city tour, and a desert safari, with dinner included. Two professors who came along with us on tour asked about our learning daily, and the discussions were truly fun. Watching the cars running in the desert was an adventure I was looking forward to. It was more satisfying and fun to watch the cars surfing and rolling on the sand than sitting inside the car.

Nights in the desert are a whole new experience. The sky looked so big. Everywhere I could see, it was just the desert and the sky. *Imagine getting lost in the desert and being surrounded by a directionless, dark night. Horrific, isn't it?*

The dinner was packed with lots of entertainment that included belly dancing, a fire show, and a stall of Heena designs where the girls rushed to get one in their hands. The camel ride was free but lasted for maybe less than one minute. I sat there outside in the desert as per what Hiya suggested to me once, to watch the stars. I sent a few images to Hiya. *What an amazing night sky!* She replied. I was expecting a few more comments from her but she wrote nothing.

I was more excited for the next day. We checked into a massively tall and gigantic structure, the Burj Khalifa. We had tickets in our hands, waiting for our turn. In sixty seconds, the lift took us to the top of the world. From the skyscrapers of Dubai Marina to the world's largest man-made palm tree, it was truly mesmerising to witness the wonderful structures in one frame by standing at one place.

I shared a few pictures with my friends in the group. One by one, they all reacted except Hiya. Something was wrong with her. I observed that she behaved differently when I met her last time. She wasn't smiling as usual and didn't talk much either.

The next day was the last day of our trip, and we had a night flight to catch. We went to explore the nearby area, including the market and mall. Dubai had so many malls and thousands of supermarkets. I did some shopping for me and my friends. By evening, we reached the airport and flew back to where we belonged.

Hiya

My classes were coming to an end. Maybe one or two weeks were left for me to enjoy Vihaan and Arnav's company, their ridiculous behaviour, lame jokes, and their way of teasing me. I didn't know about Arnav, but Vihaan was on leave. I hadn't talked with Arnav since he came back from Dubai. He showed up in the class and was carrying a backpack. Our eyes met, and we gazed at each other for five seconds and smiled. I realised that five seconds can be really long. He was back to his beardless appearance. He looked more stunning than ever in a casual teal-green shirt and blue jeans.

'Hey!' He said as he sat on the chair next to me, removed his backpack, and swirled it around that it nearly hit me, but I saved myself. His act took me back to the time when we travelled in the rickshaw together.

'How was Dubai?' I asked.

He praised the beauty of Dubai and talked about the roads, modern infrastructure, and advanced technologies. He advised me to visit the place. He gave me his phone to see all the pictures. While swiping the phone screen, the thought of his girlfriend automatically popped up in my mind. I was about to give his phone back to him when I saw a picture of him with a girl. He saw me looking at the picture.

'That's Disha, good friend of mine' he said. 'Studies with me in college.' He took his phone from my hand.

There was a chance that a good friend could be his girlfriend. I didn't want to, but I couldn't resist myself from asking, 'Girlfriend?' I regretted asking it instantly. I didn't know I could ask him such bold and straightforward questions.

He looked at me for a second and replied 'No.'

I changed my mind after about five seconds. Even one second of eye contact is enough to make you feel so many things, like instant embarrassment for asking foolish questions.

'I…' He said and I turned to him. He was staring at the monitor screen. 'Don't have… a girlfriend.' His eyes met mine. 'Never had any.' He added and later changed his sight.

I was speechless, still looking at him. My mind stopped working, like all of a sudden the production of thoughts was put on hold which is rare as most of the time I just talk with myself.

'Why do you ask though?' He asked. 'You think that I have one?'

'Yes,' I said at once. 'I mean, no. I don't know.' The way he was watching me and listening to my answer, I lost my words.

'Well, now you know,' he said with a grin.

Arnav pulled out a small paper bag from his backpack. 'Some memories of Dubai I brought for my close friends. Open,' he said, giving me the paper bag.

I pulled out a fridge magnet which had Dubai's all famous buildings crafted on it, and a small metal statue of *Burj Khalifa* from the bag. There were some chocolates too. I was overwhelmed to see the things he had brought for me and expressed my gratitudes.

* * *

I put the *Burj khalifa* statue over my study desk and stared at it. I couldn't believe that Arnav brought a gift for me. Doodle was wondering what kind of toy I got for him.

'That's for me, not for you, Doo.' I took his paws in my hand and kissed it. He climbed on the bed. I took the bag of chocolates and sat next to him. Doodle tried to snatch the chocolate from my hand. 'That's also for me, not for you,' I said.

Doodle barked loudly to show his anger. 'This is not good for you.' I showed my anger and then poured his food into the bowl. Funny how he eats the same food every single day with the same enthusiasm. I finished one Snickers bar and was unwrapping another one when a thought disrupted my mind. *Who is lying? Vihaan or Arnav?* I couldn't decide whom to believe.

If Vihaan's lying or playing one of his nasty pranks on me, then I would prefer to stay away from that boy for the rest of my life. My intuitions were telling me to trust Arnav's words.

He has the right to choose whether to express his inner world in front of me or not. But I needed to confront Vihaan once and ask why he did this to me. One after another, the thoughts were making me crazy endlessly. There are only two ways I can control my emotions: one, by playing with my doodle, and second, by listening to some high-bass music, and I needed both.

Vihaan

'The smell is amazing,' I said, smelling the perfume that Arnav got for me from his so-called educational trip.

'You must visit the place bro,' he said. 'You'll get mesmerised by the dense concrete jungle.'

'I get jealous of your college sometimes,' I said, putting the perfume in my existing collection. 'Your college takes you to Dubai and my college takes me to visit the *Sardar Sarovar Dam*.' I let out my frustration.

Risha knocked on the door in search of her laptop. She doubted me.

'If you're lying, you'll have to pay for it,' she said and left.

I pulled out her laptop from my cupboard.

'Are you serious?' Arnav said with raised eyebrows. 'Why didn't you give her?'

'Questions will be answered later. First check if she has gone down or not.'

'Why both of you can't live like normal siblings?' He murmured, following my orders. 'She is going down,' he said and we both came out from my room.

I cursed my luck when Risha all of a sudden decided to climb the stairs. She caught us. Our feet froze. Arnav ran back to my room. She looked at the laptop in my hand. Once she identified it, she attacked me like a mad lioness. I ran to her room, put the laptop on the table, and jumped on the other side of the bed. She threw all the different sizes of pillows available on the bed on me and, lastly, threw herself on me.

I raised my hands to stop her, but she snatched my hair instead. I fell onto the bed, losing my balance. I put all my good boy behaviour aside and held her hands tightly while they were punching me. She again snatched my hair, and this time I snatched hers too. Her loud scream reached my mother. I tried to shut her mouth, but she bit my hand instead.

'What are you doing?' my mother shouted. She saw me trying to shut Risha's mouth, which instantly made me the culprit. I released her immediately. My sister didn't leave any chance to make me feel guiltier. Ma scolded me very badly and beat me too. I gave Risha a sharp look before leaving her room.

'You could have just given it to her when she asked,' Arnav said as he saw me.

'She really beat me hard. Is her boyfriend teaching her all these techniques?' I said, looking into the mirror. 'Look what she has done with my hair.' I took the comb and adjusted it again.

* * *

'I'll surely spill out her little secret if she ever raises her hand on me,' I said, sitting in front of the computer, in my revolving chair.

'You're still thinking about it. Forget it, man!' Arnav advised me. 'Where is Hiya?' He asked.

'I don't know. Haven't got any message from her.' I checked my phone.

'You know that day when you were absent, she asked me if I have a girlfriend,' Arnav said. My ears and eyes, which weren't working after being beaten by my mother and sister, paid sudden attention to his words.

'What did you answer?' I asked slowly.

'Of course NO. Why would I lie?' Arnav's words hit me like an arrow. *By the end of the day, I might get beaten up by another girl. Oh god! Where is my world leading me? I hope she doesn't think that I played a prank on her. I truly care for her feelings from the bottom of my heart. I hope she takes a leave today. I am not ready to face her.*

The very next moment I saw her. I looked at her and smiled, but she didn't. The way she looked at me, I became sure that I'd definitely be found in the hospital. I wondered if she brought a rolling pin in her bag to beat me, or maybe the water bottle would split my head into two. I checked her nails in case she decided to use them as weapons. My sister's sharp nails scratched my arms. Luckily, Hiya didn't have such horrible nails.

When Naveen came in, he mentioned that we just had two more lectures and then an exam remaining. Arnav still had a month to go.

'Is it necessary to give exams?' I asked Naveen.

'Yes, you can't just get a certificate like that.' He snapped his finger. 'You've got to earn it. Right Hiya?'

'Yes, passing the exam will be proof that you taught us really well and didn't fool us,' she retorted looking at me.

Her eyes clearly told me that she was upset and might have misunderstood me. I had to clear her doubts. It wasn't possible in Arnav's presence. But my luck gave me a chance when Arnav decided to leave early to finish his work. He asked me, but I was still not ready to go home and face my mother and sister. Hiya also denied as she came late. I got my opportunity to talk with her.

Hiya and I sat there in silence for a while. She didn't even look at me once, but I was looking at her every minute. When she turned off her computer, I followed her.

I stopped her in the parking lot. 'I have something to say. Can we talk?' I asked hesitantly.

'I've to go.' She turned away. I held her wrist to stop her. 'Leave my hand,' she said, frustrated.

'I won't until you don't listen.' I tightened my grip. I could see her frustration turning into anger. 'I just need your ten minutes, please.' I begged.

She gave me a chance. We went to a newly opened sandwich shop on the other side of the road. I ordered a grilled cheese sandwich for me and fresh lime soda for her, against her wish.

'Why did you lie about Arnav? Hiya asked when I was in search of words to start a conversation.

'I…' The waiter interrupted to serve the order and broke all my confidence.

'Do you have any answers?' Her stern behaviour reminded me of the sir that came to take viva for one of my subjects. I took a deep breath and let out a sigh.

'I had no intention of fooling you.'

'Then what were your intentions?' She asked, confused.

'Will you let me speak? I am already nervous,' I blurted. She kept mum. 'I wanted to know… I mean… I had doubts that you… you've something for Arnav.' I closed my eyes at the end of my sentence.

'What?' She asked, still confused.

'You… have feelings for Arnav,' I said the last four words with super express speed.

She was awakened by my words and adjusted herself on her seat.

'Don't lie,' I said in my most convincing voice. 'If you have something on your mind, you can share it with me.'

Her hands were holding the soda glass, scratching it softly. 'Why do you want to know?' She asked. I could feel the awkwardness in her voice.

'I just want to clear my thoughts,' I said. 'Tell me it is what I think or not what I think.'

'I am not bound to answer and… That's none of your business,' she spoke, eyes gawking at the glass.

'I don't want cryptic notes. I want an answer,' I said sternly.

'Your sandwich is getting cold,' she said.

'Let it become ice. Answer what I asked.'

She kept stirring the straw. I waited patiently for her answer. 'I like being around him, spending time with him, listening to his ambitious talks, and his love for his pet.'

'So, it's true that you like him.'

She nodded slowly instead of speaking.

'So you've any intentions of asking him?'

'NO. NEVER,' she answered, promptly looking at me. 'That's out of my daring power.'

I nodded and took a bite of my cold sandwich. 'Tell me if you've a change of mind. You can trust me on that.'

She shook her head. 'Have you ever… tried to find out what is in Arnav's mind?' She asked.

'Well, He is too much involved in his career. I don't think he ever had a thought of seeing someone.' I put the last bite in my mouth. There were no comments from her. We walked again to the parking area and she disappeared soon.

I was right about everything but wasn't sure if Arnav and Hiya ever will end up living in the same story or will have an individual one.

Hiya

It was two in the morning, and I and my thoughts were wide awake. *You could have just said no, a lie straight on Vihaan's face. Why didn't you just run away? Is it even real?* I couldn't figure out what powerful source forced me to open my heart and share something that just existed in my fantastic fictional world. *How could I just let someone in with such carelessness? What if Vihaan tells this to Arnav? What if, by now, he told Arnav everything, and both of them laughed hard at my stupidity?* I imagined Arnav and Vihaan sitting on the couch, eating corn fritters in Vihaan's room, making fun of my feelings.

NO! I jumped out of my bed. I splashed water on my face and looked at myself in the bathroom mirror. *What do you think of yourself? Who allowed you to say out loud such confidential words? And why did you confess it to Vihaan and not to the one who deserved to hear it first? Arnav deserves to hear this first not Vihaan.* I conversed with my mirror image. I buried my face in the napkin and wished to take out all my embarrassments that were eating me.

In the morning, I woke up with the same thoughts. In college, I was lost in the same thoughts. I checked Vihaan's and Arnav's social media profiles for no particular reason. Somewhere in my heart, it made me happy that I just had two more lectures left and then I'll never have to face Vihaan, and on the other hand, it created an earthquake in my heart knowing that I won't get to see Arnav either.

Will I ever meet him in person again, or will he be just another person added to my social media profiles? If both of us end up living in the same city, there are chances to get a glimpse of him. What if he moves away to another city or another country? This is so hard. Why do I feel so attached? In the past few months, I've known Arnav a lot, but that doesn't give me the right to get attached, does it? I've known Vihaan too. I don't feel the same for him! What sort of nonsense is happening in my life?

The bell rang loudly and drew my attention. I put my face on the bench and covered it with my hands. Priya tapped my shoulder and asked me to join them for lunch. I refused to join her. They left after I gave an excuse that I wasn't hungry.

All I could think of was one dialogue from the movie Tangled, when the evil mother Gothel said the words, '*what have you done?*' when Eugene cut down Rapunzel's beautiful, shiny, long, golden hair. '*What have I done?*' I repeated it in my mind again and again.

All right, I'll go early today and leave early. I said to myself. I tightened my ponytail, watched myself confidently in the mirror before leaving. I read Arnav and Vihaan's faces carefully when they came. None of their faces had any suspicious expressions. Everything between the three of us seemed normal. *My ability of overthinking is expanding day by day, I must say!* Naveen was going on leave for ten days so he wanted to finish remaining lectures at once.

'What about me?' Arnav asked worriedly.

'I'll let you know once I come back then we can resume,' Naveen said, patting on his shoulder.

'So that's it. I hope you enjoyed learning with me,' Naveen said after two hours. It was past seven when he finally stopped teaching. My plans of coming and leaving early were ruined and three of us left at the same time.

'Finally, no more classes,' Vihaan said. 'I think we should party.'

'Why? Because you became a software pro?' Arnav said. Vihaan nodded.

'We can go to any fine dining restaurant.'

Both of them were busy discussing. None bothered to ask me once if I am available or not, nor my opinions. I refused when they asked me to join.

'Oh come on, Hiya. This could be the last time the three of us party together,' Vihaan said.

'Excuse me!' Arnav interrupted. 'We can meet anytime we want to. We're still friends. Her Doodle and my Cookie are lifetime friends.' I liked the way Arnav said those defensive words.

'Yeah whatever but Hiya you'll have to come,' Vihaan said.

* * *

For two weeks there were no messages from Vihaan. *Did they go alone? Have they forgotten me already?* Vihaan never said anything regarding Arnav since my confession. One day in the evening I got a message from Vihaan. He asked me if I was free the upcoming Sunday to join the party. I said yes.

I reached the restaurant on time that Vihaan told me. He had called me early on purpose.

'So, any change of mind?' He asked after the waiter served us water.

'I don't want to make fun of myself,' I said, sipping the water.

'Arnav will never make fun of such naive things.'

'Have you ever felt that he feels something for me or someone else?' I asked.

'Honestly I am not sure, Hiya. When it comes to love and feelings, he is…' Vihaan searched for words, staring at the wall behind me. '…dumb. He is a totally dumb person and will never accept what he feels for you or for anyone else.'

His words didn't soothe my soul.

'In my opinion I can say that he is going to end up in an arranged marriage if you or any other girl don't take the initiative.'

The waiter came to take the order. Vihaan told him to come later. He continued talking to me. 'However, you can try some moves if you want to know if he has you on his mind or not.'

'Like what?'

'It's upto you. You'll have to think and come up with a plan the way I did.'

Vihaan was right. *Arnav is indeed dumb. I need to think of how I can find out what's going* on *in Arnav's mind.* Before we could discuss anything further, Arnav joined us. We ordered some delicious food and later some sweet dishes in the end.

Arnav

'What could have gone wrong?' I asked my flatmate. The electric geyser wasn't working for two days. Even though it was a forty-degree Celsius temperature outside in the month of May, I still need a little bit of hot water to shower.

'I've already called the person to fix it. He'll come soon,' he spoke, looking at the watch.

I had plenty of time until the geyser get fixed. I saw the date, May 25, when I unlocked my phone. *Isn't Hiya's birthday tomorrow?* I checked Facebook to confirm, but it was hidden. I checked her Instagram profile next and scrolled down her gallery. There I saw an old post of hers that had a cake, Doodle, and Hiya in it. The date was May 26.

Happy birthday girl!!! Best wishes from me and Cookie. I sent the message at 12:00am.

Thank you so much, Arnav. Glad you remembered. The reply came immediately. I asked about her birthday plans. There was nothing special, as she had an exam to attend. *Poor girl!*

Not just Hiya, but I was busy with my exams too. I was busier than her in-fact. Later that night, I asked about her day. She and her parents visited the same restaurant to celebrate her birthday, where we had all three gone. I asked her about her dog. She got her doodle on her birthday, so they celebrated it together. She put a post on Instagram, just like previous year, with a thank-you note. In her royal blue dress, she looked so charming. I couldn't get my eyes away from her picture. She looked even prettier the night when she knocked on my door unexpectedly wearing traditional attire. My thoughts lured me to check the pictures from that night.

I couldn't get Hiya out of my mind. Every now and then her thoughts disturbed me. *Will we ever get a chance to meet again like this, apart from our school gatherings? Like the way she agreed to come with me to the beach! Will I ever get a chance to play with her Doodle?* I again went through all the photographs in which she was present, especially the one we took on the beach with her and my dogs.

Am I attracted to her? No, I don't think so. Why do I like to think about her so much? I shut my phone and thumped it on the bed. *All because of Vihaan!* I said, putting my hands beneath my head. *He is the one who planted all these thoughts in my mind, stupid Vihaan, idiot Vihaan!*

Hiya

The fourth and final year of my engineering, I'll be called 'an engineer' then. The dream tag for what we thrived all these years and now just one year behind. The tag which will give us a chance to work, to earn, and to live a life we all dreamed of.

Instead of paying attention to the first lecture of last year, I was busy daydreaming. It gave me good vibes, though. I imagined myself as an engineer, wearing a yellow helmet, inspecting the site and advising my helpers and workers to do the right things.

'Why are you smiling?' Rahul asked.

'Nothing just dreaming of myself as an engineer.'

'To make it come true, concentrate in the class please.'

'How about doing post graduation in building and town planning?' I asked him.

'Great!' Rahul replied. 'You're finally thinking of going for more studies.'

'I am not sure just looking for more options though!'

'Yes, you can look for more options according to your interests.'

* * *

It was a sunny Sunday. I took my doodle to the newly renovated park in the morning for a walk. There were a few more people like me, who came along with their pets.

'You can make a lot of friends here and we can come every Sunday, doo doo,' I said to my Doodle.

We walked a few hundred metres, and I unexpectedly spotted Arnav standing with his dog, talking with someone. I saw him after a long time, maybe more than a month. Seeing him brought a smile to my face. *Should I go? No, that's not a good idea. I don't want to make things hard for me.* I turned around and chose the opposite path.

I heard a dog barking loudly. I turned to see. Cookie recognised me instantly. Arnav was standing in front of me, shining in the bright sunlight, with his dog. I stood there in front of him with my dog. A sudden gust of wind and the flowers of pink trumpet trees joined the swirling air around us. His Cookie barked loudly and drew my attention.

'Didn't know you were coming here,' he said. 'You come every Sunday?'

'No, it's my first time,' I replied. 'But this place looks better than it was before.'

'Have you seen from the other side?' He asked, and I denied. He insisted that I join him.

'You finished your classes?' I asked, walking.

'Yes, but it was so boring without both of you.' He chuckled.

We chatted for a while playing with each other's dogs. When there were no conversations left to talk about, I took leave.

'Let me know whenever you come to this place,' he said to me, I turned around to his side and nodded.

* * *

Dear Doodle,

Sometimes, I get so jealous of you and the whole animal kingdom. Your lives are quite sorted. You come to life, eat, survive, and die. Whereas we come to life, create chaos, invite troubles, hurt ourselves with our own words, and create troubles for others as well. Half of our lives are spent complaining. Our lives are a constant struggle between what life wants from us and what we want from life.

Unlike us, there is no drama in your case until I create one in your life. I wonder if you also have two types of thinking: emotional and practical. In our world, practical decisions are called wise most of the time, and emotional decisions are often labelled as fool's choices.

I feel like my life is in turmoil mode right now. I honestly feel like living less and worrying more. I should be enjoying the last year of my college but here I am, puzzled into a chaotic world created by me. I am out of focus, and the present and the future seem so scary right now, and the past gives me a notion of comfort, and I don't want to escape from there. All those moments are soon to be a year older since I became friends with Arnav. I feel trapped sometimes, or maybe it is me who has trapped myself in it. Help me!

I met Vihaan a few days later at his request at the Phoenix Cafe.

'This is regarding you, so I am not spending any money today. It's on you,' he said, and he ordered a cold coffee. 'We're here to discuss your future husband, so…'

'Excuse me!' I gave him a sharp look. His word baffled me.

'Sorry. But… I want to know, Why Arnav? I want to know the story.'

I didn't expect such questions from him and that confused me.

'I mean I have to be sure about the girl with whom my brother will spend the rest of his life.' He chuckled.

I didn't know what to say, but I had my chance, and I needed to be honest. I had seen Arnav and Vihaan's unbreakable friendship. He won my trust that day in the sandwich shop. I took a deep breath and began slowly.

'Honestly, I don't even know how all these things started ruling me. All I know is that, when we were in school, the first time I heard his name and saw him, I felt an instant connection. I used to watch him, although I could never initiate a conversation with him, but I've spoken to him in my mind thousands of times. When we left school, I thought all these stupid feelings of mine would disappear too.'

I saw Vihaan listening to me with keen interest. My eye contact couldn't match his as I was shy, opening my heart, which I had never done before.

'I would have overcome those thoughts only if Arnav would have continued living in my made-up world.' I resumed.

'But you met your hero in real life and started having real-life conversations, right?' He said it with a smile. I admitted. 'Continue,' he said.

I then talked about the entire year's journey. From independence day to joining class together, the *Navratri* that we celebrated together and accidentally won the extra prize, the bet he won that led us to the *Dandi* beach early in the morning, the time when we missed the train and got on the bus, the time when I helped him with his drawings, the poem he wrote and showed it to me, our times in the class, our affection for dogs, and so many more moments forced me to like that person. When I was done speaking, he covered his mouth with his hands.

'Wow, my best friend hid many things from me then,' he said. 'I should have spied on him too.'

'Now, do you think that Arnav feels the same way?' I hesitated, but I asked.

'As per what he says, it's a no, but now that I've heard the unsung stories of you both, I think there are chances, but he... will never admit it.'

'What if I do? I said without thinking but regretted later.

'I see someone so desperate!' Vihaan's words put my face down in shame. 'You're so much in love, aren't you?' He said, raising my chin. He looked so happy. I blushed.

The waiter brought the bill. Vihaan took it before I could extend my hand.

'I was joking. I never let girls pay.'

'But, I want to pay today.' I snatched the bill back from him to pay.

One good friend can change your life, your perspective. I am glad that I made a friend like Vihaan. There was one more friend whom I had to tell my story to and that girl was… Kavya.

Arnav

'Lost in thoughts?' I snapped my finger against Vihaan's face.

A lot of drama happened in his life as his sister, Risha, finally announced her boyfriend in front of her parents and expressed the desire to marry him. Her parents didn't like it initially, but she convinced them to meet the boy's parents.

I was in town, and Vihaan had invited me to his home as he was alone and his parents had gone with Risha to meet her boyfriend's parents. We had plans to play games on the PlayStation. Though Vihaan and Risha fight over a silly matter, both of them care for each other a lot. I never met Risha's boyfriend, but Vihaan praised him when I asked.

'Will your parents approve of your choice if you bring a girl home?' He asked.

'I don't think they'll deny,' I said. 'But it's never going to happen.'

He paused the game suddenly. 'Why do you keep saying that?' He looked pissed off at my answer. 'Tell me, what if a girl comes and tells you that she loves you?'

I scoffed. 'Why would someone want to be with a nerd like me?' I said. 'She will eventually leave or get bored of me because I'm not an interesting person.'

'You're unbelievable.' He didn't look happy, and he resumed playing.

I paused again. 'Why is it always about my non-existing girlfriend?' I argued. 'Why you're so keen to get me a girlfriend, why not for yourself?'

He didn't reply and resumed playing. I paused again and demanded an answer.

'Has any girl ever asked you about me or do you know a girl who likes me?' I asked him sternly, as I was irritated by his same questions.

The doorbell rang, and he went to open it. His parents arrived with his sister. It was best for me to leave myself out of the family matter. My eyes met with Risha, she shook her head, gesturing that all was well.

Later that night, I got to know from Vihaan that his parents liked the boy's family and that things were on a positive note. However, they had not given the approval. One thing that kept nagging me was that Vihaan didn't answer my question, and it irked me. I wondered why he kept forcing me to get into a relationship as if he had found one for me ready to ship and deliver. *God help this friend of mine.* I sighed.

Hiya

Kavya didn't believe in my words when I told him about Arnav. 'You and Arnav!! I mean how, when and where?' She asked curiously. I narrated the same story that I had said to Vihaan. She consumed all my words with enthusiasm. We had planned to meet Vihaan at the Phoenix Cafe. There Vihaan talked about his sister, who wanted to marry her boyfriend but she still needed a green signal from her parents for marriage. There was a sudden change in the weather we noticed while sitting in the cafe.

'Looks like rain is knocking on the door again.' Vihaan said as the sky roared.

'Season's first rain,' I said. 'Always enchanting.'

They both looked at me, waiting to say more. 'Well, my friendship with Arnav grew during this season, so it's special,' I said

'When was the last time you two saw each other?' Vihaan asked.

'A few weeks ago, I went to the park with my Doodle. I found him there accidentally with his Cookie.'

'Long time!' Vihaan said. 'Let me see if I can arrange something.'

Kavya showed eagerness to know his plan. Vihaan recalled the plans we were making on Arnav's birthday, and mentioned that it was high time to execute them. We discussed a few plans while sitting in the cafe until we finished our milkshake.

I was riding back home and I remembered that my mother had told me to bring a few things from the grocery store. Just before I reached the store, it started drizzling. I rushed in to save myself.

'Can you also add a kit-kat?' I asked the shopkeeper after he put the things in the bag.

'One for me too.' A known voice I heard and turned to look.

The first rain of the season didn't just bring memories but showed me the person attached with the memories. My heart was happy to see him. I kept staring at Arnav's face thinking once again we met accidentally. I wished for these kinds of accidents to happen daily. I bought a kit Kat for him, too. He was curious to know how I ended up in his nearby area and my mouth almost revealed Vihaan and Kavya's names. I told a lie instead.

Outside the store, under the roof, eating kit-kat, we waited for the rain to stop. Vihaan was right, it's so hard to get Arnav out of his studious world. Every time we meet, he talks about studies. *Why can't he talk about something else? I am sure he isn't as shy as me.* The common quality between us is that if we don't have any necessary points to talk about, we become silent. It was the first time we enjoyed rain together.

* * *

Dear Doodle,

My mind is becoming restless. I'm unable to decide whether to exhibit my feelings to Arnav or wait for the things to magically happen which is impossible. Both Vihaan and Kavya, have different opinions. Vihaan, who knows Arnav better than anyone, believes that Arnav might not be ready to be in a relationship. On the other hand Kavya is encouraging me to give it a try. I have to hear Vihaan's opinion but I feel like I am more bent towards Kavya's advice. I hope to land in the right place without getting myself hurt.

Now that all my school friends have finalised the idea to visit the monsoon festival in Saputara, I hope Arnav will join too. He is the uncertain in the group, famous for his last minute back out. Our plan is to stay there for two days, of course you're coming with me. You're going to love the heavenly cold, rainy and windy weather of that place.

A day before, Vihaan had sent a message to the group mentioning the place from where we had to start the journey. Early in the morning, at six, we were all supposed to be there. Arnav came last with his Cookie. Vihaan came along with the driver in a tempo traveller.

The weather was just as I imagined, drizzling and cold. All the mountain tops were covered with clouds. The place was packed with people as if half of South Gujarat had come there.

Doodle and Cookie were enjoying the weather more than us. Our stay was in one of the hotels near the lake with a great landscape view. We went to relish the sunset point and had some fun activities there. Arnav had brought his DSLR camera and was busy in his own world, capturing the beauty of nature. I had never used a DSLR camera before and wanted to try my hand at it. Without any hesitation, Arnav put his camera in my hand and taught me its operation patiently.

'Take a picture of me, and I will rate your skills.' He took a few steps back, put his hands in his pockets, and posed. I took pictures of him from different angles.

'Not bad, Hiya,' he said, checking the pictures. 'You're a tough competitor.'

I blushed at his compliments.

'This one is surely going on my social media tonight,' he said, gladly.

'I want credits then,' I told him.

Vihaan and other boys who saw the pictures also wanted to get clicked. I spent nearly half an hour as their unpaid photographer. It wasn't raining, but the weather turned cold at night. The hotel management had lit small bonfires across the garden. Few were already occupied, and we sat near the one with no people. I and Arnav sat next to each other with our dogs. We all talked about random topics that came up in everyone's minds and opened up old memories. Travelling together can be so much fun, and I never knew it until I experienced it, but only when you're with your people.

Before heading back to the room, Arnav asked if anyone was interested in the morning walk. None showed interest except me and Nikhil. Everyone wanted to avail sleep in those comfy beds.

* * *

The morning was pleasant and foggy. Nikhil dropped out at the last minute, saying he would rather sleep. I and Arnav took the way towards the lake on a nice pathway, and from there we took the Saputara Point road and walked inside the big garden located on the bank of the lake. We removed the leashes of our dogs to let them stroll independently. The moment they got their freedom, they both started playing and chasing each other. We played with them, too.

I got tired running and chasing, but Arnav still had energy and kept entertaining both the dogs. At last, he sat next to me on the bench. Secretly, I hoped from him not to talk about studies. That would be the last topic I would want to talk about. He leaned his head on the backrest of the bench, exhausted.

'Same old routine to follow from tomorrow, Hiya,' he said, groaning and stretching his hands. 'I need more days.'

'You still have a full day, so you better stop complaining and start living,' I replied.

'You'll be free from studies next year. I still have one more year.'

Typical Arnav! He started talking about studies again and murmured a lot of things regarding architectural stuff.

He could have talked about movies, Bollywood, Hollywood, or something more interesting. I wasn't listening to his words.

Should I tell him? Is this the right time? Should I confess my feelings to him? Can I do this? Sometimes you have to wait for the magic to happen in life, but there comes a time when you have to become the magician and create the magic on your own. *Say it. Just say it. Tell him right now, Hiya! You don't know if you'll ever get a chance like this or not. Take a step forward and confess.* My inner voice was constantly forcing me to do the impossible. I tried to fight back, but it didn't help. I stopped Arnav from talking about his stupid college stories that had potential to compete with Hindi TV shows.

'I've something to say, Arnav,' I said, breathing heavily. My heart was pounding faster and I was becoming nervous. His eyes were staring at me. I tightened my fists. 'I… I like you.' At the end of my words, the world seemed to stop moving. I took a deep breath and let it out. 'I really enjoy talking with you, listening to you, and spending time with you,' I said, gathering all the courage I could muster. 'Do you feel the same way?' I stared at him too.

Arnav remained silent. He continued to stare at me, astonished, as if jabbed by my words. 'Hiya, I…' I could sense he was having trouble speaking. 'I… I am sorry, Hiya but…'

His few words snatched my anticipation of knowing his answer from my face. He softly placed his hands on my shoulder. Before he could say anything, I envisioned my entire world falling upside down.

'Hiya… I believe you're a very good person with the kindest heart. Don't feel bad, please, but… I'm not sure if I feel the same way. I hope you understand what I am saying. I don't know how to describe it further, but I don't want to be in any relationship right now, not at the stage to manage it.'

Arnav

She stood up. 'Hiya, I…' Nothing came from my mouth. I was numb. *What am I supposed to say?* I couldn't think of a gentle way to make her understand that it wasn't about her, it was about me. I was not as perfect and caring as her. The more I tried to make her feel comfortable, the more embarrassing it became for me.

A tear fell from her cheek, and she looked down to hide her face. Never in my life have I felt so miserable. Somewhere in a small corner of my heart, I felt happy that she liked me and considered me someone special. I enjoyed talking with her, too. I enjoyed listening to her stories, but I wasn't ready for a relationship with her or anyone else. I took her face in my hand and wiped her tears. I was feeling guiltier over the fact that I made her cry.

'I am okay,' she said, taking a step back from me, avoiding eye contact. I observed her facial motions, and nothing felt okay to me. She was hurt. She looked around in search of her dog.

'Hiya, say something, please.' I took her hand in mine.

'We're getting late, Arnav.' She released her hand and continued looking for her Doodle.

We saw our dogs sleeping next to each other comfortably. I was still hoping she'd say something.

'I had no intention of making you feel uncomfortable,' Hiya said, tying the leash. She walked past me. I took my Cookie and chased her.

I blocked the path by standing in front of her. I saw a tear in her eye again, ready to roll down. I slowly took a step ahead and embraced her. 'I am a horrible person. It's not true that I don't like you, but getting into a relationship is not the right thing for me right now,' I said and freed her from my clutch.

'I understand, Arnav,' she said, adjusting her hair strands that had come out with me.

We walked together to the hotel in silence. Vihaan saw us in the hotel lobby with our dogs. He advised us to get ready before check-out time.

We all spent a half day in Saputara, had lunch, and did some shopping. I kept checking on her to make sure she was okay, but she avoided all possible eye contact. We returned to our town late at night. Everyone was exhausted and wanted to go home. I and Hiya were the last to get off with our dogs.

She stopped me. 'I think none of us is guilty, Arnav. Don't worry. I am fine,' she said. We both exchanged artificial smiles. 'I should have listened to Vihaan, and all these wouldn't have occurred. He knows you like no one else does.'

My fake smile stopped in the middle. 'Vihaan?' I said, perplexed at how his name came up in the communication.

'Actually, he found out that I… like you,' she smirked.

That's it. After that, I couldn't focus on her words. I couldn't believe that Vihaan knew and yet let it all happen, making me the bad guy. *How could he, and why did he never tell me?* The more I thought about it, the more enraged I became. Hiya went home with her father, who came to take her. All my friends had also gone.

I saw Vihaan making financial settlements with the driver, a few feet away from me. I watched him with anger boiling on my face.

'We need to talk,' I said, peacefully, as I approached. Vihaan gave the payment to the driver, and he left. It was eleven in the night. There were very few vehicle movements, and there were no people around us. I tied my dog's leash to the pole, away from him.

'Did you know that Hiya… likes me?' It was awkward to speak, but it didn't affect my anger. Vihaan was startled and tongue-tied.

'Arnav, I…' Before he could say anything I grabbed him by his collar.

'Listen to me, please,' Vihaan urged. I was in no mood for a fun talk. Someone was hurt because of me.

'Do you realise what fuss you've created? How could you, Vihaan?' I shouted and tightened my grip.

'Wait a minute, did she confess?' Vihaan asked worriedly.

'Yes, she did, and thanks to you, who provoked her and supported her,' I shouted furiously and pushed him away. He saved himself from collapsing. He looked at me angrily and pushed me back with more force.

'I never told her to confess it to you, and I would have stopped her if I knew,' he roared angrily. He grabbed my collar. 'And if you remember, I warned you a long time ago to stay away from her for her. Did you care to listen?' His rage was becoming stronger than mine.

'But you could have said sternly to her not to confess it to Arnav,' I said, releasing myself and pushing him away. The dispute heated up, and we continued throwing accusations at each other. We almost beat each other in the middle of the road.

'You've hidden so many things from me, Arnav. There were times when you and Hiya were alone, spending time together. Am I wrong, brother?' He said furiously. His allegations made me uncomfortable. 'It's not me. It's you who created this mess for yourself and for her as well.' He pointed his finger at me.

'It's not all my fault,' I said, trying to maintain my peace. We convey our anger through our eyes. 'You could have saved all these from happening.'

'All right.' He shook his head in arrogance. 'You know what, its your life. Do whatever you want. I don't care, and I don't want to see your face,' he said, stabbing his finger on my chest. He stormed out the next minute, angrily.

When I was alone on the road, I thought about Hiya and hoped she would be alright and wouldn't be drenching her soul in tears. I went home with Cookie, who was barking constantly watching me and Vihaan fighting. I'd never spoken to Vihaan harshly ever. I covered myself with guilt that night. I hurt a girl and misbehaved with my best friend, and I realised that it was all my fault.

* * *

I didn't receive a single text or call from Vihaan. I was so embarrassed to face him. It affected me in my studies as well. A part of me wished for Vihaan to take the initiative and sort out things between us. A week passed without any communication. I decided to see him. One night, I knocked on his door with two pizzas and coke tins, and luckily Vihaan opened it.

'Wrong house. I didn't order pizza,' he said firmly, closing the door. I stopped him.

'It's a new arrival, sir. Try it, please,' I said with a smile, and I forcefully entered. His mother saw me and welcomed me.

'I've had my dinner. You can leave and enjoy eating alone,' he said sarcastically.

I didn't care to listen and continued talking with his mother. I met his sister and father as well, who were watching reality show on television. Vihaan climbed the stairs to go to his room. I followed him and dragged him to the stairs of the terrace. I climbed on the concrete water tank and forced Vihaan to do the same. I opened the pizza boxes. He refused to eat but later gave me a grumpy look and took a slice.

'I am sorry,' I said, finishing one slice. 'I overreacted.'

He didn't respond and took another slice. 'Say something.' I got irritated.

'Apologies accepted only because you brought cheese burst.' He looked at me and then smiled. I chuckled back. A burden from my head was dismantled. I took the credit for sorting it out. We mocked each other until we finished one pizza.

'I need a favour,' I said after a while. 'I want you to check on Hiya if she is ok. I don't have courage to speak. Will you?'

He thought for a while, drinking coke. 'At your service, anytime!' He said. 'But tell me one truth, do you feel the same way for her?

I looked at him. 'Yes,' I replied. Vihaan would've undoubtedly seen me as the stupidest person on the planet. 'I like her too, but saying yes would not be the right thing.'

'Why do you think so?' He asked worriedly.

Saying yes to her would probably escalate her expectations of me. The situation I was in demanded focus instead of love, a focus on my life, my dreams, and my ambitions, and I wasn't in a position to handle both. I never found myself capable enough. I explained my views to Vihaan, and he understood well that it would only make things worse.

'Tough times and life are waiting for us, brother!' He said, taking a sip of coke. 'In the next ten years, we'll finish our studies, start working, and maybe have chances of getting married as well. So many adventures await us.' Vihaan showed the reality so far.

'Slow down. We're still kids,' I said.

'No, imagine being married! It terrified me too,' Vihaan said. 'One day, you'll be married to a girl. She will be everywhere. You'll have to share everything, like your house, room, cupboard, bed, bathroom, everything!'

His terrible narration scared me. I imagined Hiya in my bedroom, trying to rule me and make me obey her commands. 'No way!' I said, gulping my coke stressfully. 'Will I have to take permission to meet you?'

'We'll lose our freedom. There will be no personal space.' Vihaan said worriedly. I requested him to change the topic or stop scarring me. We sat there in silence, looking at the night sky.

'My father was asking if I've any plans to go abroad for further studies,' he said.

'You said no, right?' I replied quickly.

'I haven't thought about it. But…'

'You're not going anywhere. The decision is taken,' I said sternly. 'If you don't want to spend the rest of your life being my hostage, you better say no.'

'You love me so much, don't you?' Vihaan put his hand around my shoulder, pulled me and teased me. 'Are you willing to be my permanent room partner?' He laughed loudly.

'Shut up.' I grabbed his neck and bent him down. He apologised instantly. I released, and he adjusted himself.

'Your presence matters in my life,' I said. I saw him listening to me carefully. 'I need you more than you need me. I want you to be there, celebrating my success and comforting my sadness,' I said, taking the last portion of my coke.

'I'm not going anywhere, Arnii,' Vihaan said sincerely. He collected empty pizza boxes and Coke cans. 'You'll find me first standing next to you always, promise!'

I shook my head. I knew that I could count on him blindly. He will be there for me even before I call. I am blessed and lucky to have him. The years we've lived together since childhood have become so constant that watching him going away from me would gradually kill me from inside. I know that I matter equally to him and this bond would never let us live apart.

'I've applied for internships at a few companies,' I said.

'Where?' Vihaan asked curiously.

'Surat, Ahmedabad, and Mumbai as well,' I replied. 'Mumbai is my first choice.'

'Minutes ago, you were telling me not to leave, and you already have plans. Such discrimination!' He turned his face.

'I am not going to settle down there. I'll come back once it's over.'

When we were done talking and eating, we came down.

'Will you be able to see someone else holding Hiya's hand?' Vihaan asked, and my feet stopped moving. I never thought of seeing Hiya with someone else.

I turned to him. 'I just have to say… She will remain mine if she is destined to be mine.'

Vihaan

Arnav had given me the responsibility, and I had to fulfil it. *She could have at least informed me before getting down on her knees in front of Arnav. I could have handled the situation better. What made her exposing her feelings all of a sudden? It was shocking for me too. I never thought that she would do it without my help. Brave girl!*

I decided to meet her. She wasn't ready to meet me and made a lot of excuses. I was stubborn and went to her house with an excuse to exchange the notebook. She was shocked to see me in her house.

'Can we go to your room, please? I need to talk.' I buzzed in her ears. Her mother brought a glass of water, and I took a step back. Her dog appeared out of nowhere. I used Hiya as my shield and hid myself behind her. She handled the situation and we went to her room.

'I am surely going to get a dog bite for free, serving you and Arnav,' I said. 'You both will have to pay my medical bills.' She tossed the book on the bed and asked me my reason for the meeting.

'You know, I got beaten by my best friend because of you.'

'What?' Her irritated face suddenly turned worried. 'I never meant to create a dispute.'

'No one can create a dispute between us, remember that,' I said, reading her anxiety.

She apologised to me and asked why I wanted to see her again.

'Consider me your pigeon, but Arnav wanted to know if you're ok.'

'Stop lying. Why would he ask?' She turned around and sat on the bed.

'He did. Believe me.' I sat next to her.

'Tell him I don't need his sympathy.'

* * *

'Did she really say that?' Arnav asked, surprised. 'How could she?' He said, confused.

'I support her,' I said. Arnav was stunned. 'She is a strong headed girl.'

'I thought she…'

'…Will never get over you? Is that what you think?' I asked, throwing my attitude. 'You're not a prince charming. Come out of illusion.'

'Stop assuming,' he raised his voice.

'Then leave her alone. She'll definitely find a better person than you.'

Arnav didn't respond to my sarcasm. *Good for him. Then only he'll realise what he did.*

Hiya

When Vihaan asked me about how I was doing, I lied to him that I was okay and it didn't affect me. But that wasn't the reality for me. Yes, Arnav's choice made me cry so badly, but I respected his decision. Life gives everyone a chance to make choices, and we are free to choose what we want. But those choices have the power to leave a deep impact on the people, who are closer to you. I think about it often: *what if Arnav had chosen to accept me?* We would have been together for three months. I try not to think about it, but I can't control my overthinking mind. It forces me to think about the moments I could have lived with Arnav. *Why do I like to keep hurting myself with the same painful thoughts again and again?* Sometimes, these thoughts make my heart happy, and then the same thoughts make me cry. *Is this how love feels like?*

I often met Vihaan and Kavya. It sometimes amazes me how Vihaan managed to keep an honest friendship with me all these time. When I told Kavya about what happened in *Saputara* between me and Arnav, she consoled me and checked on me every now and then. Though I never expressed how deeply all those things affected me, neither to Vihaan nor to Kavya.

On a cold December evening, I went to the Phoenix Cafe with my college friends and found Vihaan sitting there. He saw me and approached. I introduced my friends Rahul, Priya, and a few others to him.

'Arnav will be here soon,' he said. My heart skipped a beat. I hadn't seen him in four or five months. To run away wasn't possible, as my friends were waiting for me to join them. The bell attached to the door rang. Arnav, in a black leather jacket, a white t-shirt, and blue jeans, entered. He was looking for Vihaan but saw me instead. We continued looking at each other from afar. I moved to join my friends. They took their seats. From where I was seated, I could see his face, and he could see mine. Our gazes locked many times, and we both changed them promptly. I left the cafe first with my friends.

'Hiya.' Arnav came out following me. I asked my friends to go. 'How are you?' He asked. I shook my head in reply. 'I want to apologise… for not keeping in touch. Whatever happened, I had no intention of severing our friendship in this way. I didn't have the guts to talk.'

I listened to what he said calmly. He seemed to have had these phrases suppressed in his heart for months.

'I got selected for an internship in Mumbai,' he said.

'Congratulations!' I said and extended my hand for a handshake. 'Best of luck.'

I began walking, as there was nothing else left to say. He stopped me again. I turned around. He had something to say but couldn't let it out. I bid my goodbyes to him. I took a few steps ahead but turned again. 'Happy Birthday in advance, Arnav!' I said. My wishes brightened his face with a grin.

* * *

I laid on the terrace floor, under the night sky, with my Doodle. The sky was clearer than it was last week. The count of visible stars was higher. *I'll buy myself a telescope with my first salary, Doo.* I said patting Doodle's head gently.

I checked my phone to get the exact location of the planets and searched the sky. Except Doodle, no one knew how many tears I had shed in the last few months. Whenever I had my heart full of sorrow, I came to the terrace. I talked and cried in front of the stars. I blamed myself for setting my expectations too high. It was all my fault to imagine a world that had no chance to become a reality. My mind ran so much ahead of time that I forgot to check the present scenarios. I blamed the stars for not writing my story the way I wanted them to. It all turned out to be a big lie. All my despair compelled me not to believe in the story of the stars.

Arnav

I took the morning train to Mumbai. It was going to be a life-changing experience for me. I had visited Mumbai several times for pleasure but had never lived there. Living and surviving in Mumbai is difficult, and I knew it wasn't going to be a smooth ride. The metropolis never sleeps, and people are always on the go. I landed with a heart full of high hopes.

I had made all of the arrangements for my stay in advance. I dropped my luggage there and rushed to the office. I was nervous on my first day in the professional world. I had dressed appropriately. I completed the formalities and was handed a desk with a computer system. The 32-inch TV-size monitor screen blew my mind. *Working on this big screen would be so much fun!*

So many feelings jumbled together; I felt awkward, encouraged, delighted, and anxious. The people around me were very knowledgeable. I had to remind myself that I was still a student and not a professional architect. I made friends who were newly joined but they had a degree in hand. At night, I expressed my experience to Vihaan. He assured me to visit Mumbai wherever he gets a chance.

Every day was a new learning experience. The office atmosphere was enthusiastic. On weekends, I used to have fun with my teammates. Days and months passed easily with them. I went home a couple times to make sure Cookie didn't forget about me. Vihaan was busy with his final year project. Life was keeping both of us busy but we managed to meet each other a couple of times. When Vihaan finally planned to visit Mumbai, I introduced him to my teammates. We had a plan for a party.

After a long time, I finally got to speak with Vihaan face-to-face. We chatted about everything from college to our favourite shows, sports, and politics, and, lastly, about Hiya. It's not like I never talked to her in the past few months; we talked through messages, but it was brief. Vihaan was keeping me updated about her, as they had met a few times.

'She asks about you every time,' he said, enjoying the exceptional view of marine drive. 'Life and time never wait for anyone, Arnii. In my opinion, you should reconsider your thoughts.'

I was speechless. The waves crashing on the tetrapod, filled the silence between us. She never left my mind, either. Long time had passed since I saw her. He looked at me for answers despite knowing that I had none.

'A big reunion is being planned as in two months we'll be getting our engineer's degree,' he said. 'I and Nikhil are contacting our other schoolmates apart from our group for the party.'

'I still have one year left,' I responded. 'I'll see if I can manage to come or not.'

'To keep the bond alive, we all must meet every once in a while,' he stated. 'We haven't gathered since our last trip.'

A long time passed since that never-to-be-forgotten trip, Hiya's unexpected words, and me becoming the heartbreaker. I wished things hadn't turned out like that on that day. Hiya would still be my friend, and we would have continued to share dog-training advices, listening to her unusual topic, her passion for stargazing and finding planets at night. *Hiya! I want to see you.* My heart desired.

Hiya

'You look so pretty, Hiya!' Kavya complimented my white floral dress when I met her at the graduation party. I appreciated her.

The party was planned by Nikhil and Vihaan. The decorations were beautiful and the arrangements were done perfectly. I met Vihaan and praised his hard work.

'You look lovely,' he said, embracing me. 'Arnav might go blind as I'm sure he won't be able to see anything except you.' He whispered in my ears.

'Is he coming?' I asked, without any curiosity. He nodded. Nikhil summoned him and he left me and Kavya alone.

We sat with other girls. The banquet hall was filling up fast with people. Nikhil mentioned that there were a few fun games he and Vihaan had planned and would start once everyone arrives. My phone rang. I went outside to talk as the music was playing loudly in the hall. It was Rahul who called me regarding a job opportunity. I followed my habit of walking while talking and toured the entire place, including the stairs. I cut the call after fifteen minutes and climbed the steps again. My silver bracelet fell from my wrist. When I collected it back, I saw that, out of five stars, one was missing.

The bracelet was gifted to me by my parents and was my favourite. I searched the entire place. *It could be somewhere on the stairs, too.* I scrutinised each step carefully. My heels missed the last step. I was saved before any part of my body could get fractured. My eyes were closed tightly just as my firm hand gripped on the shoulder of my Saviour. I opened my eyes cautiously and loosened my grip, which might had left a scar on the person's shoulder. I saw a face that I never wanted to see for the sake of my naive heart. Arnav let go of his hand, which he had wrapped around me.

'Looking for this?' He said it while staring at me and opening his fist. I saw the star I was searching for.

'Yes,' I said, taking my hands off him. He was standing close to me. 'Thanks for saving me and for this.' I showed the star and took a step away.

Vihaan saw both of us entering the hall together. He came forward and hugged Arnav. 'Thanks for coming brother!' He said.

Nikhil gave a funny speech as a starter. He advised us to have dinner first before playing games. I avoided every possible contact with Arnav, but he kept gawking at me every now and then. *Maybe Vihaan was right.* But there was nothing new in me worth staring. I had worn a simple dress and had my hair cut. After dinner, boys sat on one side and girls on the other for dumb charades. However, taking part wasn't mandatory. After that, a few people took part in musical chairs. Then they all played fun games we used to play on sports days in school. I stood there with Kavya, cheering them up.

At last, the DJ man played high-bass beats. I'd never seen Arnav dance so madly where as I sat on the chair, being the complete opposite person. I saw Vihaan coming towards me, dancing. I started denying it before he could reach me. He held my hand and dragged me, using his physical strength, into the pool of dancing people. I stood there like a mannequin.

'Put your hand around my neck,' he said into my ears. 'If you want to see Arnav's jealous face.'

I felt awkward but followed his words. I saw Arnav watching us. 'Now smile.' He swirled me around and pulled me closer. Arnav had stopped dancing and was continuously looking at us. I looked at him frequently to see his reaction.

'You know, I know him better, so I can clearly say that he's jealous,' Vihaan murmured.

I saw Arnav gawking at us, and the jealousy on his face satisfied me. Together Vihaan and I took full advantage to annoy Arnav. The party ended late.

'I'll drop you home,' Vihaan said when he saw me calling my father. Arnav was standing with him.

'You'll be needed here, as you're one of the organisers,' Arnav said. 'I'll drop her.'

Vihaan agreed easily. He looked at me like he wanted this to happen or that it was part of his plan. Vihaan hugged me again, showering gratitude for coming. I saw Arnav getting uncomfortable watching us.

I didn't talk much in the car except the answer I gave for his questions. He narrated his experiences of his internship and Mumbai life. I listened sincerely. We reached home. Without more interaction I wished him *good night* and he left. I slept so peacefully that night after months as two good things happened that day, one was meeting Arnav after a long time and second, the way he couldn't take his eyes away from me!

Arnav

She has changed a lot. Since when has Vihaan became so close to Hiya? I knew that they were meeting regularly, but their closeness was infuriating to me. Did she forget me? She doesn't like me anymore? She didn't talk to me at the party and ignored me like I wasn't there. Vihaan's behaviour is out of character. He should not be with her. It should be me.

Did I just consider myself with Hiya? I thought about her every day in Mumbai, and I became a non-existent person in her life. Why? How?

* * *

I was sitting in the college canteen one day, eating noodles.

'My gratitude to you. You deserve a treat from me.' I heard someone talking. The voice seemed familiar. I checked around. I saw two people sitting on the other side of me. I couldn't see the girl as her face was in the opposite direction. I checked the bracelet and identified it. *That's Hiya! What is she doing here?* My eyes rolled at the person sitting in front of her. *Who is he? What is she doing with him? Why is she in my college? Is she applying for post-graduation?* They both seemed to be talking like old friends. I turned away my face when they passed by me to throw the paper plates. *'See you next week.'* I heard Hiya.

What to start from next week? Does Vihaan know? Even if he knows, I can't ask him. I'm sure he'll throw awkward lists of questions at me instead.

* * *

A week later, at the same time, I went to the canteen in the hope of seeing her. I waited long enough, but she didn't come. I checked the civil department, which was next to the architecture department. She was not there. *Why am I being so desperate? But she could have at least informed me. Is it a sign she doesn't consider me a friend now?* I was walking towards my department, lost in thoughts, when I bumped into someone. He was the same person talking with Hiya that day.

'Sorry buddy, I was in a hurry,' he said. 'My friend is waiting for me.'

Yeah, Hiya, coming. He informed it on the phone and ran. I wanted to run behind him, but I had an important lecture to attend. *Why is she becoming so mysterious? Has she found someone special?* Coming out of the last lecture, I spotted Hiya and the same guy walking together near the civil department. I followed them and stood behind one of the pillars at a safe distance.

'Thanks Rahul once again,' Hiya said to him.

Rahul, I've heard this name, but when and where? I recalled our conversation on *Dandi* Beach, where she mentioned him as her good friend. Watching them talk and smile didn't give me the vibe of *just* good friends.

* * *

I was coming out of the stationery shop when I saw Hiya entering college. Looking into her phone, she was walking in my direction. I didn't move. When she noticed me as an obstacle, she looked up. I pretended to see her for the first time, whereas my eyes had been on her for the last month. She greeted me warmly.

'I got a job as a professor here,' she said. I investigated that a long time ago. 'It's contract-based, though.'

'Good! See you around,' I said, throwing a fake attitude, and was about to leave when someone joined us.

Hiya introduced him as Rahul, her friend from college.

'I am going home today. Want to join?' I asked her.

'Actually, I have to attend the wedding of a college friend, and Rahul will drop me off.'

The fact that Rahul and Hiya will go in one car together at night ached my heart. I controlled my emotions and left them alone before my insecurities could explode.

I was packing my bags, recalling my day. Every now and then, I couldn't stop and think about Hiya. *What would she be doing? Is she having fun with Rahul?*

My phone buzzed. *If you haven't left, we can go together.* That was a message from Hiya. My heart rejoiced. I agreed and suggested she meet me at the station. We mutually decided to take the last local train. The train was on time!

I was waiting for her at the entrance of the station. I thought she would come in a rickshaw, but she came in a car with Rahul. For the first time, I saw her in a beautiful red and yellow saree. I couldn't stop myself from looking at her. We walked to the station together. She complained about how difficult it is to climb steps in saree wearing heels. She almost fell once, but I saved her.

'Is falling down the stairs became your hobby or what?' I took the bag from her hand so she could climb properly. She removed her high heels before taking other steps.

'I shouldn't have agreed to wear it,' she said.

'Weren't you supposed to go with your friend?' I asked her. 'What changed your mind?'

She stopped on one step and said, 'I changed my mind.'

'What about your ticket?' I asked. 'I'll get one for you.'

'I am a first class passenger now,' she said.

We smirked, reminiscing about the bus ride. We sat on the platform next to each other, waiting for the train. She was busy with her phone, and I was submerged in the thought of how pretty she was looking in her outfit. The open hair suited her which she had curled. She removed her earrings, bigger than her size of ear and massaged it. I wondered how she managed to wear such heavy things on her tiny ears for hours.

The train arrived. I let her climb first, making sure her saree won't get stuck. The first class was almost empty. We both chose the window seat, facing each other. It's completely opposite in the morning, when I hardly find enough space to stand.

'Why have you never told me that you got a job at my college?' I asked.

'I never wanted to join,' she said slowly. 'Rahul's brother works as a professor, and he recommended me.'

'You look more like a student than a professor.' I scoffed. 'Does students even listen to you?' I mocked.

She chose to look out of the window instead of replying. I wanted to keep riding in the train so that I could gaze at her more but our station arrived so soon. It felt like the local train moved at super-fast speed. Vihaan was waiting for me at the gate. He saw us coming towards him. Hiya's father had also come for her. After she left, Vihaan looked at me with a big question mark on his face.

'No questions please, I am tired,' I said and sat in the car but told him the whole story the next day.

It took a while, but Vihaan's parents were finally on board for his sister, and she was finally going to get engaged. There were still two months left as per the auspicious time. Vihaan had invited every member of the school group. He had arranged a fun night a day before the engagement. Surprisingly, he invited mine and Hiya's dogs, too.

In college, mine and Hiya's paths used to cross daily. She wasn't ignoring me anymore, but she talked very little. We often met in the canteen, and sometimes Rahul, her friend from college, used to join us too. He got his admission for a master's degree at the same college. I realised after talking with him that he wasn't the bad guy. I talked with him many times and found that he was a clever and focused student. Hiya, a sweet and beautiful little professor, was a favourite amongst students. It looked funny to see her surrounded by students taller than her.

I offered my service to pick her and her Doodle up for Vihaan's fun night. She didn't refuse. When I went to her home, she was getting ready. I waited for her in the living room. Doodle and Cookie, who met after a long time apart, easily recognised each other. Doodle rushed to the stairs, and my Cookie ran to chase.

I got worried as my Cookie hadn't been to anyone's house before. It would've looked awkward to run into someone else's house to chase my dog so I informed Hiya's mother about my situation. They both had ran into Hiya's room. Hiya was overjoyed to see Cookie. Her look reminded me of my days of software classes, when she used to wear casual jeans and a top with a ponytail. In college, I mostly saw her in Indian wear only. She looked beautiful in whatever she chose to wear. She was ready to go.

'I forgot my bag,' she said on the stairs.

'I'll bring. You take these both and stuff them in the car.' I said, handing both dog's leashes to her.

I found her bag placed on her study table. I saw a few pictures of little Hiya that were framed and were hung on the wall. It brought a smile to my face thinking how cute she looked as a kid. The same kid with whom I studied in the same school for twelve years watched her become an adult but never talked. When I took the bag from the table, a few things fell on the floor. I put the bag aside to collect it. My eyes stopped on a paper with something written on it. I took it in my hand to read.

Let me cry for a while,

Coz my world doesn't seem right.

I am supposed to get up and fight,

But all I do is cry and cry.

Lots of things are ruling my mind,

I wonder why you left me behind.

Without you, I don't feel fine,

And I am so lost all the time.

My sun will only rise and shine,

The day I'll proudly call you mine.

But now when I look up in the sky,

The stars show me stories of lies.

I have hope that one day you'll heal these scars,

And make me believe in the story of the stars.

I read it two more times without caring that she was waiting for me. *She really loves you, Arnav! Do I deserve to be loved this much? What made her love me this much?*

I folded the paper and put it in my pocket. Vihaan's house was beautifully decorated on the outside and inside. The ceremony was to happen on the terrace of the home with a limited number of guests. We danced, sang songs, and ate so much food. Amidst the fun, I kept recalling Hiya's heartbreaking writings. I could feel the misery behind her smiley face every time I saw her.

After partying for two hours, we laid down in one room. Vihaan played a movie and brought popcorn and chocolates. One by one, everyone fell asleep except me and Hiya. She went to the garden. I took some finely wrapped chocolates and followed her. I saw her sitting on the swing. I sat next to her and offered her chocolate. The night was silent, and only bugs were chirping.

'Do you know that there are hidden messages inside of every wrapper?'

'Really? You open first,' she said, taking one from my hand. I unfolded the wrapper and put the chocolate in my mouth first. *One place you haven't visited in years.* I read.

'So, where is that place?' She asked.

'The place… I used to visit my village as a kid with my parents. There was a big pond with a small hill next to it which anyone could climb easily. That hill was famous for its gorgeous sunset. I haven't visited there in a long time. As a child, it was magical to see the sun's reflection in the pond.' I looked at her after answering. She smiled and unwrapped her chocolate.

Sleep under the stars tonight. She read. She smiled and looked up at the sky. 'We're already under the stars.'

'Want to go to the terrace?' I asked cheerily. 'The arrangements are amazing.'

'Let's go!' She murmured excitedly.

We entered with our dogs on the terrace. I looked for the switches and turned them on. The yellow string lights illuminated. Hiya was standing in the centre, shining bright. She stole all of my attention. My eyes were stuck on her like magnets.

'How will we see the stars with these lights on?' She muttered. I obeyed her advice.

I took some cushions from the sofa and placed it on the floor. We laid our heads and stared at the sky silently. She showed me visible planets.

'What is so fascinating about stars for you, Hiya? I asked, watching the sky.

She exhaled deeply. 'I've been looking at stars since I was a child. The shiny scattered pearls in the wide sky used to amuse me, and they still do. Years passed and I grew up, but my habit stayed with me. Certainly, my thoughts about stars changed. As a kid, I believed in the theory of people becoming stars after their death, but I involved myself in science, which taught me what stars really are, a giant floating orb made of mysterious rocks. I often think about the presence of life on other stars, or may have lived on those stars once and witnessed the apocalypse the way our dinosaurs watched their existence being wiped out. It thrills me to imagine such things.'

She pointed her fingers at two random stars. 'Imagine those two stars talking to each other about their day, how fast and far they travelled and how far they still have to go, gossiping about how the lives living on them and ruining its beauty, what difficulties they faced, and how many asteroids attacked them.'

I kept humming and smiling at the end of her silly sentences. She continued saying ridiculous things that only she could imagine. 'So you're saying that stars live like us? I turned to her side, pulled my face up and rested it on my palm to see her speaking.

She looked at me. Her face was glimmering under the moonlight. 'When it comes to the universe, nothing that you imagine is wrong.' She replied. 'Universe is equally dangerous and beautiful.'

'I believe you,' I mumbled. We looked at each other. I gently put my hand on hers and rubbed my thumb.

'What's so special about me, Hiya?' I asked in low voice. 'Why did you choose me?'

'You've always been special to me, regardless of any reason,' she said. 'All I know is that I like to be with you.'

'You're so perfect, Hiya,' I whispered.

'So you are Arnav for me,' she said.

'In our school days, there was a girl in the class whom I found so beautiful and I was attracted to her,' I said. 'Do you know who was she?'

'Who?' She asked.

'That girl was you.' I said. She stared me, astonished.

Amidst silence, I took my face closer to hers. My hand sensed that she had tightened her fist. The closer I got, the faster my heartbeat became. I could feel her breathing getting faster. I rubbed my nose against hers. I attempted to go closer. My lips almost touched hers.

'This is… wrong, Arnav,' she spoke softly, putting her hand on my chest to stop me.

I slowly dragged my face away. 'I am so sorry.' I turned away. She got up from the floor and sprinted away with her dog, leaving me behind with my embarrassing thoughts.

* * *

The more I avoided thinking, the more I ended up thinking about that night. I wanted to tell Hiya to erase that moment of my dumb attempt to kiss her. *I should have taken her permission first before taking my face closer! At least she stopped me at the last moment gently instead of slapping me! I have never been hit by any girl's hand till date.*

It was my move, and I'll never be able to forget that. I never felt such desperateness. I wondered what forced me to do such a shameful act. When I saw Hiya in college, I behaved awkwardly. I was so embarrassed that I changed my directions every time I saw her. She called me in the canteen one day, and her comfortable words removed my agonies. After chatting with her for an hour, I felt so good. From that moment on, I realised that losing her would be my biggest defeat.

Choosing a life partner is as important as choosing the correct career path. Vihaan was right about the twenties being full of pressure. There are lots of hard and permanent decisions we have to make in this decade of life. *I have to confess before I lose her.* I knew someone who would eagerly want to help me.

* * *

'You what?' Vihaan was flabbergasted when I confessed to him that I almost kissed Hiya, on the terrace of his home. It took him a lot of time to consume my words. He kept repeating *you kissed Hiya* and I kept correcting him saying *I didn't.* I wasted a lot of time explaining to him.

'My studies will be finished soon, and after that, I want to make one more decision,' I said to him once he was convinced that nothing happened between me and Hiya.

'What is that?' He asked.

'I want to confess my love for her!' I said. 'You asked me one question, and my answer is that I won't be able to see someone else holding her hand.'

Seeing my dedication, Vihaan gave me a tight hug. 'I knew that you'd realise it one day, buddy.'

I discussed my plan with Vihaan, and he was equally excited. I decided to execute my plan after my graduation.

I maintained my contact with Hiya until then. Hiya decided to go for post-graduation after completing her contract based job. I felt like everything was falling into place. I finally decided to make her mine forever. I asked Vihaan to make arrangements until I brought Hiya to that special place.

I had already convinced her to spend an evening with me after the last day of her job. I took her to my special place, the small hill in my village, to witness the gorgeous sunset. We sat there till the sun stopped glimmering. She enjoyed the sunset, and I enjoyed watching her.

When the sky grew gloomy, she prepared to leave. I quickly sent a message to Vihaan to turn on the lights. She was taken aback to see the view of thousands of scattered tiny lights covering the hill. She was also sparkling with a broad smile glued on her face.

'I tried my best to bring the stars to the ground for you,' I said.

'This is so beautiful,' she exclaimed, running in all directions. 'It's like I am floating in the sky.'

I dragged out the paper that I had stolen from Hiya's room and put it in her hand. She opened it.

'From where did you get it?' She asked, surprised.

'I never knew that someone could love me so much apart from my parents and Vihaan,' I said.

I clasped her hands. 'Hiya, I am twenty two years old. I just finished my bachelors and will definitely be applying for masters. I have a lot of things to achieve in my life. But I deeply believe that finding a life partner is as important as choosing a correct career path.'

I pulled her hands to my face and kissed her fingers. 'I found that partner in you, Hiya. You are my indeed need. Losing a girl like you will be my biggest failure. I respect your dreams equally as mine. I promise to be there for you when in need.'

Her eyes were filled with tears with a small grin on her face. I pulled out a small box and got down on my knees. I opened the box which had a silver ring with a star on it. 'Hiya, the stars have come on the ground to fulfil your wish, to make you smile, to bring the change you want in your life, and to make you believe in the story of the stars.'

She couldn't hold back her tears of happiness. Watching her, my eyes became moist too. 'Please accept and wear this one more star I brought for you. I want you. Do you want me too?'

'Yes!' She said, crying. 'I want you, always!'

I stood up. 'This has no diamonds on it nor is it made of gold but I'll get you one someday, I promise,' I said showing the ring. I held her finger and slid the ring into it.

'This is all I want,' she said, looking at the ring. She embraced me the next moment. I grasped her more tightly. The warmth of her hug was so soothing.

I adjusted her hair that came out with me. I put my hand on her cheek and kissed her forehead.

'There is something which was left undone,' I said nervously.

'What?' She asked.

'Just don't push me this time,' I said and pulled her closer, leaving no chance for her to take a step back. She shut her eyes as I drew my face closer to hers. I closed mine too and kissed her. She wrapped her hands around my neck and kissed me back.

'Excuse me! Sorry to interrupt you,' We both heard someone and took our steps back immediately. 'Kissing in public is illegal in this country. I hope you know!' Vihaan said.

Hiya was shocked to see Vihaan. She looked at me.

'*Bhabhiji!*' Vihaan came forward happily and wrapped her in his arms. 'Finally!' He swirled her around by lifting.

'Put her down!' I shouted at Vihaan. He hugged me next and did the same act. I could see the happiness overflowing from his face.

'Now, you two will have to help me in order to convince the girl I saw a few days ago,' Vihaan said.

'Who is she? What's her name?' Hiya asked, eagerly.

'She is newly joined in my father's company,' Vihaan said. 'Her name is Vihaana.'

I and Hiya both were stunned on hearing the name. We looked at each other and released a big laugh.

'Vihaan's Vihaana.' Arnav laughed. Vihaan made a grumpy face. We found it funny but assured to help him.

Epilogue

'It's time, Mr. Mehta!' Vihaan said.

'It's been five years already, I can't believe that,' Arnav replied, looking at himself in the mirror.

'Well, today is the day when all the wait ends.'

'I am feeling the same nervousness of the day when our parents met each other. Life has changed so much in the past few years.'

'And both of your parents agreed in the first meeting. Relax. There is nothing to worry about now, Arnav,' Vihaan said, pacifying his worries. 'I know that whatever comes, you and Hiya will always remain together.' He tapped Arnav's shoulder.

'How is she looking? You saw her?' Arnav asked curiously.

'Beautiful and fascinating as always,' Vihaan replied. 'You must proceed before she decides to choose me as her groom.' He chuckled.

They both proceeded to the marriage venue. Arnav saw Hiya with her bridesmaid Kavya. Hiya, in her red and white wedding attire, was doing a photo-shoot with her Cookie and

Doodle. Cookie was now more close to Hiya than to Arnav and he could never dare to raise a complaint against her lady. Arnav watched her from afar, smiling every time Hiya smiled.

Hiya's sight finally caught Arnav, gawking at her. She walked near him. Arnav held her hand and kissed gently.

'Hiya Naik, I am proud to have you,' he said.

'Let's have a photo-shoot,' she said and dragged him. They clicked several pictures with their dogs.

A bunch of people came and took the groom and bride away as the rituals were to begin. The wedding stage was decorated elegantly with string lights of shining stars and some flowers. Arnav sat on the stage. The priest began the ceremony and started chanting mantras and after a while he asked to summon the bride. Hiya made her entry with her parents and her dogs. She sat in front of Arnav. A few moments later, the priest removed the partition made of curtain placed in between bride and groom. He announced the completion of rituals. Both Hiya and Arnav looked at each other with bright smiles. They both exchanged the garlands. Vihaan and the whole school clan popped the party poppers and showered flower petals.

Arnav held her hands. 'Many more miles to go.'

'To the new beginning!' Hiya grinned, came forward and kissed Arnav's Cheek.

www.ingramcontent.com/pod-product-compliance
Lightning Source LLC
Chambersburg PA
CBHW021350150726
47989CB00005B/2177